Poison Ivy

Written by: Tania Coulter

Cover Photo provided by: @dirty_gal_diana

This Book is dedicated to:

King & Raleigh! My nephew and niece will forever be my motivation, even if they don't know it.

Auntie Nene loves you!

Acknowledgements

Taking the steps to achieve certain things in my life has always been a struggle for me. I continuously let things distract and discourage me from obtaining my goals. No one even knew I loved to write. If at this moment a few years ago, I would've laughed if someone said I'll be a published author. All that to say; only you can make your dreams come true.

First and foremost, I would like to thank the man above. Constantly praying and asking him for strength to get me through each day, better than I had the day before. Listening to my prayers and letting me know that all things are possible.

To my three Queens! My mother, Yvonne. My two sisters; Shakira and DiAnna. THANK YOU!! These are the women who raised me into the strong woman I am today. They gave me everything raw and uncut. Only rewards were when I got the job done. Pushing me until I produced something GREAT! I thank them for just being in my corner at my lowest points and never giving up on me. Only people to recognize my talent before I did.

One time for my partner in crime, Najah. I thank you from the bottom of my heart for holding my hand the entire way. None of this was possible without you. Please don't ever change the heart you have Na, it'll take you places. I am grateful to have you. Also a special Thank You to Marcus. Thank you for loving me even when it was difficult. I LOVE YOU!

To all my family and friends I truly appreciate the continuous support. I'll try and make you guys proud. A Big Shout out to my Life Coach, Taneesha (Bukky) The universe led us to one another at the right time. I thank you my friend for helping me over that hump, your help has never gone unnoticed. THANK YOU ALL!!! I LOVE YOU GUYS!

Introduction

We're all so use to reading books about a twelve year old girl being sold to the highest bidder by her mother for a small crack rock. Or a sixteen year old boy, having to neglect his hoop dreams to slang drugs to provide for his infant siblings because his mother's hours got cut short at work. Having a drug dealer for a boyfriend is the popular thing. Stripping to pay for college is the norm and buying foreign cars becomes regular when you got money in the hood. Some people can relate to all of the above but let's discuss something that everybody can understand besides the drugs, cars, clothes and money. What happens when envy and jealousy meet up with betrayal and have a party?

Chapter 1

Growing up it was just me, my mom's, and our cat Lucy. My mom wasn't a whore but she wasn't a saint either. I guess she just liked to entertain men from time to time. Mostly the landlord who came on the first of every month because he knew she didn't have the rent. You know the classic story; Mom turned tricks to keep food in our stomachs and clothes on our backs, blah blah blah. Wait, I guess you can call her a whore! I respected my mother because she made shit happen. I never went without as a child and I mean never. But all that seized on a cold winter morning. Lounging in bed all day was at the top of my "to do list". Anything that required me moving could kick rocks. I didn't move from that bed for hours, forgetting that life even existed outside of those four walls. Finally deciding to jump back to reality is when shit hit me hard. Walking towards the bathroom, I called out my mother's name and didn't get a response. It was weird that she had not checked on me all day but shit she must've needed some "me" time just like I did. Rushing into her room to see if she was sleep, I felt in my gut something was wrong. On several occasions I would wake her up and put her in her bed after she had been partying all night long but something about that morning just wasn't right. I screamed her name but she didn't budge to tell me leave her alone like she normally does. I walked in and immediately ran to call 911. At 8:47pm, they pronounced my mother dead. I didn't even know she had AIDS.

Clearly my mother had a past that I knew nothing about and it had finally caught up with her. We didn't have any family so it was always just us two as far as I can remember. I visited my father's mother from time to time but that's it. My father had died when I was born in a car crash. So my grandmother was the only living family I had and she didn't hesitate when they asked did she want custody. I was her first grandbaby and she would kill anybody who tried to take me away. Living with my grandmother was a pain in my ass literally. Her old ass didn't let me take a shit in peace and anything else went out the window. To her nothing I wanted to do was civilized. I remember her signing me up for some support group for teens whose mothers were dead. I missed the shit outta my mom but a group of strangers wasn't bringing her the fuck back so me being at those meetings were pointless. The only thing good about going was me meeting my bitch, Nicole.

Now Nicole was a crazy, funny ass individual. She didn't give two shits about nothing or nobody; literally. Her appearance was totally opposite of her attitude. She resembled a young Zoe Saldana, medium brown skin, tall with an active physique and the longest curly jet black hair. Her cheeks would get Rosie red when she was embarrassed or mad about something. She rarely smiled so that's what drew me and everybody else to her wondering what was hidden behind her frown. We didn't live too far from one another but we both lived different lives. Nicole didn't have a fair childhood like mine. She bounced around from group and foster homes for a while. She didn't speak about her mother at all but she enjoyed all the wild stories I shared about mine. We would always argue about me not appreciating my grandmother and how people would kill to have my spot. Being a few years apart, I viewed Nicole as the big sister I never had. Sharing every secret I could spill to her because she was the closest to me besides my grandma. Me on the other hand, I was a tall petite little thang. I danced whenever and wherever I heard music. My smooth coco skin was blemish free with a million and one freckles. All I did was smile showing off my pretty teeth and outrageous personality. My grandma May called me banana, something I've learned to love growing up. My thick black hair was cut short like Nia Long back in the day, just because I hated the maintenance that came with long hair. Some say we were friends because we were different, but I felt we were the same in most cases; sort of like sisters.

Chapter 2

Inhaling and exhaling a thick cloud of smoke, Ivy sat and daydreamed about her sunbathing in Peru or watching her children learn to snowboard in the Aspens. She drifted between fantasies as she took pulls from her blunt. Nicole interrupted her afternoon routine by continuously blowing up her phone. "Yes, my obnoxious friend, what do I owe the pleasure of this phone call? Ivy answered sarcastically. "Bitch you ain't gone believe what just happened" Nicole said in between chuckles. "What you do now yo?!" Ivy knew she was about to hear an ear full. "Ok so, Riq had spent the night with me. He been was suppose to leave but this nigga ride was taking forever. So Jay comes and texts me saying he'll be here to get me to take me to work. So I'm all hype now blushing and shit but this nigga Riq still laid across my bed as if he's paying bills in this motherfucker. I'm completely pissed right now, so I'm walking through the apartment in hopes that he catches a hint to get the fuck out. So then I peep Jay texted me again and he's telling me he's outside. "OH MY GOD BITCH!" What you do? Ivy couldn't stop laughing. "Vee, I was pissed I started sweating and shit. All I kept thinking was damn he pulled up quick as shit. Nicole had to catch her breath because she couldn't stop laughing either. So this nigga Riq still there asking me a thousand questions. I was ready to leave his ass there and just tell him to lock my doors when he rolled. So then his phone started going off. Bitch! SAVED BY THE FUCKIN BELL. I ain't ever been so happy in my goddamn life when he hopped up off that bed". Ivy was laughing so hard she had tears coming down her eyes. "So Riq's walking out the door and Jay's calling my phone now cause my two minutes turned into fifteen. Soon as I answered this nigga says "Ayo Riq lives in here?" Bitch I died. I just kept saying who? Who? I don't know who that is! Here I come though. "Nic, he didn't ask you who bul was though. Oh my goddddd" Ivy kept screaming "Vee if I'm lying I'm flying bitch" they both laughed hysterically. "But wait that ain't the fucked up part though. Bitch I gets in the car real calm like "Hey Baby" this nigga comes out and says "you wouldn't lie to me Nic would you? I kept a straight face like "huh? Babe you trippin" they both started laughing uncontrollably. "Yo he then said I asked you a question, now answer it" when I say that shit turned me on bitch" Nicole continued laughing. Ivy couldn't believe Nicole. "But wait did they speak to each other is the question sis". "BITCH WHAT?! I DON'T KNOW, I HOPE NOT" they both sat trying to fight their laughter. "We can laugh now but that shit was not funny earlier. I thought he was gonna smack my dumb ass. The lord was on my side today" between tears and laughter Nicole still couldn't believe she almost got caught up. She actually loved Jay and would be so hurt if she lost him.

Nicole started ranting and raving about her newest boo and how she wanted to settle down. Half listening now, Ivy cut her girlfriend off. "Girl, I don't understand, you talk this talk every time a new nigga comes around. Have a seat Nic. Ivy spoke in one breath. "What the fuck does that mean? So you're the only one who's supposed to be walking around here all lovey dovey and shit? Especially with a nigga who fucks around on you with half the city and I can't?" Nicole fired back in defense mode. Laughing out loud, Ivy couldn't hold back because her girlfriend needed a reality check. "Sis, I know my man ain't shit, just like you ain't shit. But here's the difference between us two. I have accepted the fact that I'm dealing with a cheater and I handle that shit accordingly. But you on the other hand, have not accepted the fact that you don't give a fuck about nothing and that's cool. I hear you talking about change but never see it sis. As a matter of fact, you just told me a story of you almost being caught by both your niggas, right?! My point exactly! You're on the phone babbling about a nigga named Jay and you just got done fuckin Riq. You see now what I'm talking about? You can't say you want one thing but do another" Ivy took a pull of the blunt before she got out of her car. "I'm only telling you this because I love you but you gotta get ya shit together before it's too late. Hanging up in the bitch's ear, Nicole was vexed. She hated how judgmental Ivy always had been and how she tried to read her like some old dusty book off the top shelf. Fuck her and how she feels, I don't comment on her fucked up situation so don't chime in on mine. Laughing even harder, Ivy tucked her phone after Nicole banged on her and walked back into the building. Ivy was way past tired of entertaining Nic's shenanigans when it came to these fuck boys. Every month it was a new dramatic drawn out story that she didn't even finish reading till the end.

Like always Mik had my simple ass out the comfort of my own home. Nicole was absolutely correct when she spoke on how my nigga ain't sugar honey ice tea and quite frankly, I was becoming fed up. Some girl he sold a dream to was just on my line claiming she was gonna kick my skinny ass when she seen me for dealing with her man. The perks of dealing with Mikel.... Parked on a small dark block, the soft music from the car radio suddenly made me tired. I could hear Usher singing about hurting the love of his life in the background. My emotions started playing hopscotch and I was rather sure my own boyfriend was somewhere doing the same exact thing he was singing about. "So he still has yet to answer my calls or respond to any of my text? I thought as I yawned. It was the dead of winter and Mik had me bundled up in a car waiting for him once again. The dash said it was 2:56am. "Why isn't he answering when I just talked to him twenty minutes ago?" Something wasn't right but I had no time to figure it out. Starting my engine up, I pulled off into the brisk night air speeding down the Street. Laughing silently to myself, I wondered what bullshit excuse he was gone spit to me when he finally did decide to call me, Typical Mik Shit! My mind was racing a mile a minute as I drifted way back.

Across town, Nicole set mesmerized by Jay's presence. Everything he did fascinated her, she couldn't help herself. He was like no man she's ever been with, he made her happy. Nicole was wrapped in his spell and didn't plan on leaving his world anytime soon. She didn't plan on speaking to Ivy for a few weeks and she was fine with that. All she needed at this point was her man "she isn't the only bitch who can keep a man" she thought as she prepared dinner for Jay.

Exhausted from the night before, Ivy awoke to her cell phone ringing off the hook. She just missed the call. Silently thanking the Lord she didn't have to work today, she checked her missed calls. No missed calls from sneaky ass but she had over ten calls from a random number. "this better not be a bitch calling about Mik's trifling ass or its on" Calling the number back about five times it kept coming back busy. Giving up and tossing the phone onto her bed the buzzing started again "Who is this?" Ivy said in the nastiest tone.

   "You have a collect call from" Mik!" an inmate at.....

Ivy instantly busted into tears as she accepted the call with a mouth full of questions. Mik heard the fright in her voice and tried to calm her down. "Baby, they're tryna say I offed a nigga" Mik laughed as if they were insulting him with the charges. "MIKEL WHAT?!" Why the fuck are you being charged with murder? Slowly closing her eyes, Ivy prayed this was some sick joke; he was forever playing. This damn sure isn't the road my mom wanted my ass to take in life. "Baby I promise I didn't do anything they're accusing me of. Just a case of mistaken identity. My lawyer will be here later and everything will be fixed. I'll be out before you know it." All the good shit you wanted or needed to hear from a nigga in jail, Mik spit it all on that fifteen minute call. "Ivy just roll with the punches babe" Mik said lightly.

Chapter 3

Days turned to months and I was doing the time with Mik. Go figure. Ordering an apple martini and some wings, Ivy sat at the bar finishing up some paperwork. She frequently came to the restaurant about twice a week after work for some alone time. She knew the waitresses and the bartenders and even some of the other regulars. So when a new face showed up she could spot them with her eyes closed. Jazz, the butch bartender, came over with another drink. She explained to Ivy that the gentleman at the end of the bar brought her another round and picked up her tab. Declining his hospitality, Ivy continued with her paperwork and ignored Mr. Mysterious. I guess he didn't like rejections because five minutes later he was totally invading the space that Ivy was in. "Excuse me bartender, I'll have another long island and get this beautiful young lady whatever she was drinking" Ivy wasn't impressed in the slightest but she did notice his scent and his teeth. Shit he was handsome, too fuckin fine but he'll never know. He was tall, very tall and had this dark bronzed chestnut skin and the cutest dimple in his chin. He didn't have extra facial hair but that was fine because he didn't need it "Nice to meet you, I'm Jace" he extended his right hand only to get left empty handed. "Ivy" she said snotty. "Feisty huh? I can work with that" he smiled "work with? I think not! Ivy turned up her nose. Jace smirked digging her attitude. "So you come here often" "Why? She shot back like she was offended "Damn sweetheart, I'll leave you alone" Signaling for the bartender, Ivy felt bad she didn't mean to come off as a bitch.

"My bad, Jace is it? I didn't mean to come off rude. I just had a very long day at work" Jace sat back in the chair somewhat relieved because it was something that he liked about her as soon as she opened her mouth. Four martinis and several shots in, Ivy was blushing and cheesing from ear to ear like a girl being asked to go to senior prom with the hottest nigga in school. She didn't know if it was the alcohol or her just being horny, but she wanted to see how Mr. Mysterious got down. Flirting back and forth for the past two hours was getting Ivy hot, and she decided it was time to roll. Letting him outta her sight was not an option at this point and she hoped he felt the same way. Taking the lead out of the restaurant, she whispered in his ear "so are we taking my car or am I getting in with you?" "Get in; I'll bring you back in the morning to get yours" Cool?" "Yes!!" She tried to hide her excitement. Heading to Delaware they continued to flirt as they smoked a blunt that Jace had already rolled moments before. The weed started to take a toll on Ivy and before he knew it she was reaching over to unfasten his belt. Giving him everything she had she wasn't letting up.

Between the martinis, weed and Mik being gone, Ivy didn't know how to act. She went all out. Pulling up to his condo, he didn't even wanna disturb her while she was at work. Leading her through the front door, no words were exchanged. Clothes just came off and Ivy fucked this nigga like her life depended on it. She licked and sucked every inch of his brown body literally, and she went wild when he returned the favor. Ivy was floating on cloud nine and nothing was bringing her down, not even the person who was blowing her phone up. She made sure her ass was printed in every room in that condo. There were no traces of a woman living there and even if there was, he was hers for the night and sis would have to catch up with him tomorrow. Finally making it to the bedroom, Ivy passed out forgetting about any and everybody. Awakening to the smell of food, Ivy had to adjust her eyes. For a second she thought she was dreaming, and for a moment she wished she was. She came back home with the cutie from the bar and rocked his world. As if on cue, his tall fine ass walked in the bedroom with a plate full of food. "This nigga aint cook for me yo" Flattered to say the least, Ivy ate a piece of bacon and asked him could they leave. "I'm sorry I would love to stay and chit chat but I have to go". Granting her wishes, he drove back silently to her car. Rather embarrassed, she kindly thanked him and hopped out his truck as fast as she could, praying that she never saw him again. She started her car and left him in the dust. Totally forgetting about her phone going crazy last night, she felt like shit when she heard the phone ring and seen that it was Mik calling once again.

Speeding home to wash and change, Ivy couldn't stop the giggles. Replaying last night's events in her head, she couldn't believe she got out of character like that. "What if he thinks I'm a hoe?" Ivy was so happy until she heard her phone ringing and her whole mood changed. Mik had been calling her nonstop since last night and she had to think of a quick believable lie to feed him. "Why the fuck haven't you been answering the phone? He shouted as soon as the operator was done telling me that I was being connected to an inmate. "I had too many glasses of wine and I passed out" Ivy said casually. It actually wasn't a lie, she did have a few cocktails, and she did pass out but she skipped the part about her having a stranger's dick in her mouth and that was the reason she couldn't talk. "You were supposed to be here an hour ago, tighten up" Mik said before he hung up on her. Sprinting into her apartment, she could smell Jace's scent as she stripped out of her clothes. In the steaming shower she explored her whole body. Imagining him standing behind her tracing his index finger over her soapy body. Feeling herself getting aroused she quickly snapped out of her fantasy and put some pep in her step. Two and a half hours and a few disrespectful C.O's later, Ivy was finally walking to the back to see her man. As she searched for Mik's face she couldn't picture her life being like this. To her left she noticed a woman and a baby boy, no older than two years old crying hysterically because they didn't wanna leave the man's side. Sitting herself down, she overheard the young man in front of her telling his mother that he doesn't think he'll be home for a long time. This place was depressing. Before Ivy could get comfortable, Mik had a bullshit story to tell like every other day. She let all that shit go in one ear and out the other. His promises always turned to memories and his apologies just were words spoken to make the situation better. Tuning Mik out like always, Ivy made the decision at that moment that today would be her last time being searched to visit anyone, not even her man.

Leaving the prison, Ivy couldn't understand the warmth between her legs. Her body was withdrawing from the amazing time she had the night before. Jace's dick was like that first hit of the pipe, and she needed another hit.

"Baby it's yours, I'm yours...

If you want it tonight...

I'll give you the red light special...

All through the night"... Ivy sang as she thought about calling Nicole to tell her what a whore she had been. Forgetting they weren't speaking, she dismissed their beef and called her friend but got no answer. Ivy started thinking about how Nicole had always answered her calls when she had to tell her some crazy shit she had done...

"Nic, I gotta tell you something but please don't be mad at me!" Ivy whispered so her grandmother couldn't hear. She was petrified but had to share her secret with her best friend. "What you do Ivy? Get some dick? Nicole yelled out while laughing. Ivy's whole mood turned from sad to happy in a matter of seconds. "How you knowwwww? Ivy was overly excited. "Cause I seen you and Hassan funny looking ass creeping back in ya grandma house after she left for work" Ivy started giggling and blushing because she was right. "But Nic why you ain't tell me dicks were so ugly?!" They both bust out laughing".

Chapter 4

I've been looking all over the city for you Miss, call me! Jace!"
Ivy couldn't fight back the big smile that snuck across her face.
Positioned in the same spot she had met him, sat a dozen of red
roses. For the past three weeks the bartender said that a dozen
of red roses were delivered with the same note that was left on
this particular day. He sent them in hopes that she would
receive them. Ivy intentionally didn't return to the restaurant
for her "me time" routine, with hopes that she would not run
into him again. Embarrassed that she even took it that far with
him made her super nervous and to top it off, she still had a
man. She grew some balls and finally sent a message keeping it
very short and brief "Thanks for the Roses!" Sipping on her
drink she became anxious as to what his response would be. He
instantly responded with "on my way". "NOOOOO, oh my god I
don't wanna see him right now, this wasn't in my plans for
today" she became tense and jumpy as if this man wasn't just
inside her a few weeks ago. Swiftly grabbing her things and
downing her drink she made a quick dash to the exit trying her
hardest to be gone by the time he got there. She was quick but,
not quick enough because she bumped right into him as she
made her way out the revolving door. "Damn you was just
gonna leave?" he sounded disappointed. Ashamed that she

tried to sneak off, she made up a small lie telling him that she just wanted to put her roses and things in the car. A small smile crossed his face because he knew she was lying. "Do you need any help or can you manage without me? I've gone three weeks without you, I think I can go another" she teased. Jace couldn't stop smiling. She had a pep talk with herself as she walked back into the restaurant. "Only one drink Ivy, and don't let him touch your hand or knee or none of that affectionate shit". She really wanted to jump into her car and ride off into the sunset but something kept her there. She didn't know what it was but it was something. "Next time can you leave a glass slipper Cinderella" he smiled. He stood up to pull her chair out. "Mik bitch ass never pulled my seat out" was the first thing she thought as she sat down. Thinking back, Ivy's face grew with worry...

Ivy and Nicole were seated at the bar enjoying themselves. Ordering food and drinks to get the night started. Laughing and giggling at the guys who tried to holla at them. The liquor started to kick in and the girls felt good. They abandoned their seats and headed to the dance floor. A few guys had come over to join them. Innocent fun was all it was. But when Mik walked into the spot, he didn't view it that way. He quickly walked over to Ivy, gripped her up by her neck and drug her out the place. The men and Nicole tried to help but Mik was a madman and pushed them all off of him. Nicole grabbed their things and followed them outside cursing the whole way. He had Ivy pinned up against the wall and Nicole lost her fucking mind. "Get ya stupid ass off of her" Nicole went to go hit him but he blocked it and just walked off. Ivy tried holding back the tears but they came down like a waterfall. Beating your ass in public isn't cool Vee like on no level. I don't know why the fuck you keep accepting the shit this bum ass nigga does. Like are you happy with the way he treats you? You can't be yo. You can't "screamed Nicole.

"Thank you" Ivy smiled back at Jace. At this point she didn't feel guilty about anything she was doing. In fact, she felt great about everything that had happened. For so long she accepted the bullshit from Mik and knew that everything was wrong, but now all the small stuff that Jace had done felt so right. They discussed everything under the sun that night. Their careers, politics, family, and a host of other things. Something she had never done with Mik's dumbass.

"So now that we've gotten to know each other more, when can I see you again? Or do I have to send out a search party this time? Jace smiled. "No that won't be necessary!" He gave her a kiss goodbye and shut her car door. She really didn't want the night to end but she would be on his line very soon.

It was a sunny afternoon and Jamila met Ivy downtown for lunch. Jamila was their girlfriend from high school. They actually met because they were dating the same boy and found out about each other. Remember back in the day, when you would three way call your boyfriend with the chick he was cheating with on the line? Well that's actually how they met and been friends ever since. Talking about everything and everybody, Ivy prayed that Jamila wouldn't bring up her trifling ass boyfriend. But prayers don't always work because two seconds after the silent prayer, she brings his ass up. "I've been tired of all the bullshit, we had some okay times but the bad days still haunt me. I loved him with every inch of me but something isn't right and hasn't been for a very long time. Girlfriend I'm happy he's locked up because it's giving me the chance to move the hell on". As Ivy sat and talked, she felt like the weight of the world had been lifted off of her shoulders and she was finally shaking this nasty habit, as if she's been on drugs for years. "I'm planning to just ignore him in hopes that he'll get the picture." Not really interested in what Ivy had been saying because she heard this sad song too many times, Jamila changed the subject "You've talked to Nic? I've been calling her but she's been real short with me when she does answer but most of the time she's been letting my calls go to straight to voicemail. Recalling their last phone conversation, Ivy noticed that she did come off a little too strong this time but she needed to let her friend know

19

the truth. I wasn't being malicious or purposely trying to hurt her feelings I would never, but Nicole had to step up and take full responsibilities of her actions. "Naw I haven't talked to her in a while, we had a little disagreement and I've just been giving her some space. I'll call her later and see what's up with her. Knowing her she's laid up with the new nigga she was talking about settling down with, who knows"...

"Why did I open my mouth? I should've just waited till I was further along, he would've been happier" Nicole sat crying in Mrs. Price's arms. Spilling the tea to Jay about her being pregnant turned out to be the wrong thing to do. She thought he would be excited about the good news being as though he always talked about children; or was it that he just didn't want any by me?

"What's wrong with me? I don't understand. It's like I can't find a guy who wants to be with me. I'm tired. I thought Jay was different. Ivy always has a guy, why can't I? What's wrong with me?" Nicole repeated as she held onto Mrs. Price. "I thought this was what life was supposed to be about. Having a husband, making babies, you know a real family. You know how I watched you and Mr. Pete live throughout the years." She sobbed loudly. Mrs. Price sighed; she hated to see Nicole being hurt. "No baby girl, it's about living your best life, stress free and happy." Mrs. Price was Nicole's foster mother and throughout the years they grew pretty close. She could always tell when something was wrong even when Nicole refused to admit it but this time Nicole needed to be consoled and Mrs. Price vowed she would always be there for her. That previous morning, Nicole had an appointment at the local Planned Parenthood to get the baby aborted. Jay was in attendance and was more supportive than ever. Leaving the clinic, Jay was quiet and Nicole was devastated. Dropping her off to Mrs. Price, he kissed her goodbye and told her he'd be back later on that night. Later turned into days and days turned into weeks and weeks turned into never. Slipping into a depressed state, Nicole lost touch with herself and everyone around her. Aborting the baby and then Jay disappearing took the other half of Nicole's heart. Knowing Nicole's in's and out's, Mrs. Price knew when she had not been taking care of herself. Her behavior becomes disorganized, impulsive, irritable and just plain mean. So hearing this story about Jay, she knew Nicole was hurting inside and knew something terrible might surface...

It was rather cold this morning, Nicole had awoken to use the bathroom before all the other kids woke up and used all the hot water. Being in the bathroom for a good twenty minutes, she returned to her room and noticed several of her hygiene products were missing off of her bed. She heard faint giggles and knew one of the jealous bitches touched her shit. Calmly *walking through the house she asked each child had they seen her things. They brushed Nicole off and laughed like she lost her mind. Quietly walking back to her room, she dressed quickly. Several moments later, loud banging noises could be heard throughout the house. Nicole had went and got Mrs. Price's baseball bat from behind the front door and came upstairs and broke every last thing on each of the girls dressers. She screamed the whole time and when she was done, she went in her room and shut the door. The children were petrified and never touched or spoke to Nicole again. Outraged and in desperate need to get to the bottom of Nicole's anger, Mrs. Price contacted the doctor who had evaluated Nicole years prior. Five days later, Nicole was diagnosed with mild paranoia and bipolar depression. Mrs. Price wasn't a fan of drugging children, but she had no choice when it came to Nicole. It's either give her these antidepressants or suffer from the consequences of her illness.*

Chapter 5

"Yeah man I know what the fuck she looks like. That was her!"
Mik had been going back and forth with his man for a good ten
minutes. He was explaining to Mik that he seen Ivy hugged up
with a basketball player type nigga. He hasn't talk to her in over
a month and this news started fuckin with him even more. He's
been calling and writing her but hasn't received a response. She
would usually come see him twice a week and now she just
disappeared off the fuckin planet. Mik wasn't feeling this not
one fuckin bit. He hung up the phone, frustrated he dialed her
number and continued to get the answering machine. Walking
back to his cell, he wished he could ring her fuckin neck for
playing with him right now. All the fucked up things that Mik
had done in the past were catching up to him slowly but surely.
He couldn't help but to think that he was somehow being
punished for all the lies he's told, the people he fucked over and
just overall the lives he messed up. He sat on his bunk and kept
pushing the idea that Ivy must have gotten fed up with all his
bullshit games and finally left him. He then thought of his
father...

"Mikel, Mikel, get back up here for daddy gets you" his sister Michelle yelled at him. At this point, Mik didn't give a shit about what his dad would be mad at. In his eyes, he didn't have a father. Just a drunk dude who beat on him and his mother. Ignoring Michelle's pleas, he headed towards the front door to make his exit. Instantly feeling a strong force against the right side of his face, he let out a huge scream. Turning around, there stood his crazed maniac of a father. Mikel lowered his eyes and noticed the steel pole his father was holding. Feeling the blood trickle down his neck, he went wild. Rushing his dad, he went straight for his throat. He tried with everything nerve in his body to choke this piece of shit to death. Unsuccessful, his father slammed him and started kicking and laughing. "You think you can beat me motherfucker? Try it." Mark yelled continuously laughing. Mikel tried looking to see if his sister was in sight to help but she was nowhere to be found. Mark stood over Mik like they went twelve rounds and he got his victory by knocking him out. Calling him all types of faggots, he went to lift his foot to kick Mik in the ribs, but he was met with a 38. Mik had saved up his allowance money and the change he got from bagging groceries to buy the gun. His eyebrows frowned and his eyes turned cold. He had had enough of the physical and mental abuse of his father. His intentions were to use it for protection on the streets but now he didn't even feel safe in his own home. Mark wouldn't stop laughing at Mikel. "You ain't got enough *heart to kill me boy" Mik closed his eyes and went to squeeze the trigger. Seconds later, he heard his father let out an unforgettable shout. Smiling and satisfied with his own boldness, Mik opened his eyes and noticed his father huddled over. Confused and scanning the scene, he saw his mother lying motionless on the floor by the front door. Regret was all he felt as he watched his father cry for the first time in his life.*

Hanging up with a client, Ivy had glanced at a picture of her and Nicole in Mexico she had on her desk. They haven't spoken in months. Nicole had no clue that she left Mik and got into a relationship with Jace, and Ivy didn't know shit about what Nicole had going on. Jamila would tell her bits and pieces of how she's been but, she didn't want to continue to keep hitting her up for information on her own best friend. We're all grown and have lives to live and things going on personally, that's life, but going this long without talking wasn't cool. Making a mental note to call Nicki and break the ice, her grandmother called interrupting her thoughts.

"Banana, Nicole just left here looking for you, she got all chubby. She ain't pregnant is she? I didn't wanna ask" Ms. May said all concerned. "I don't know grandma, I haven't heard from her in months" Ivy said dryly so her grandmother could get the hint to not ask her anymore questions. Thinking it was strange that she didn't call her cellphone she just pushed the thought into the back of her mind and continued to listen to her grandmother talk. "Well baby, give her a call, y'all are sisters and don't need to be fighting" Ending the call, Ivy just didn't understand Nicole half of the time or why she did the things she did. She gave up trying to figure Nicole out a long time ago....

Visiting Nicole in the hospital was extremely hard. Her face was black and blue and one of her eyes were swollen shut. Realizing that this only happened because Nicole always been about herself. And if you didn't like it, LEAVE! That was her motto. Anyway, her recent stunt was lining her actual boyfriend up to get robbed. Like this guy was on the verge of proposing to her scandalous ass. Long story short, she met a Chicago playa who was in town visiting his folks. A small fling turned bad. Nicole convinced this nigga to rob her own man because he didn't buy her a pair of shoes when she wanted him to. Let's just say the guy never made it back to Chicago and Nicole is lucky she still had her legs to walk.

Things started getting serious between Jace and Ivy. In a matter of months, they had done everything under the sun. She moved in with him, totally abandoning her apartment she had with Mik. Ivy never intended to jump from one relationship to the next but shit happens like that sometimes. Jace and Ivy were snuggled in bed together. Watching old black and white movies, Ivy was babbling about how she wanted to start a family.

Expressing to her man that it was too early but that's what she wanted in the near future. They both took a stroll down memory lane for a second reliving all of the best and worst times they had growing up. Jace got quiet, holding back the tears. His brother crossed his mind and he couldn't believe that he wasn't here anymore. These same streets Ivy didn't want to raise their children in took his only brother. A part of Jace had died that morning when his mother called with the bad news. Tuning back into Ivy rambling about baby names, he just agreed with everything she said. "You're right! Well can we start making this family now?" he joked as he grabbed and kissed her face passionately.

Chapter 6

Sitting fixated on why Nicole didn't call, Ivy bit the bullet and broke down and called her. "Nic, wassup?" Ivy tried to check her temperature when she answered the phone. "Bitch, I was at grandma's yesterday, where you at? Nicole replied as if they had spoken five minutes ago and not five months ago. "On my way home to my man" Ivy said matter of factly. "Aww shit Mik came home? I know you hype!" Nicole shouted happily. "Eww no, fuck Mik. I finally left his nut ass alone chile". Nicole was completely shocked. "Whattttt?! Who would've thought you'd break away from that spell he had over you!" "Girl, Jace broke that spell." Ivy laughed. "Bitch who the fuck is Jace? Oh see you done up and changed on me." Nicole was blown away at how swiftly Ivy's life was going compared to her shit show. "No hoe, I've called you to tell you what was up but of course you probably had a dick in ya mouth". They both laughed. Nicole wasn't about to share her fucked up news with Ivy so she could yell and say "I TOLD YOU SO! FUCK NO!" Her thoughts lingered back to Jay, she snapped out of her daydream when she heard Ivy speak his name. "Huh? What you say? Nicole waited for Ivy's response. I said where is Jay? "Oh girl, that nigga was cray cray! I had to leave his ass alone. He was real overprotective chile, always asking me where I'm at and who I'm with. You know I ain't use to answering to no damn body. Bitch he popped up at my job once because he thought I was lying about being there." Nicole continued to feed Ivy a bed of lies just so Ivy wouldn't have the chance to talk her regular shit. "Damn bitch, now I see why ya ass got ghost, bul had you in hiding." They both cracked up again. "Well wassup, let's do happy hour tomorrow?" Nicole eagerly asked. "Yeah that's cool. Ima call Jamila and we can make it a date. Ivy was so happy to talk to her friend she forgot what her and Nicole was even beefing about.

It was close to midnight when Jace's phone started ringing off the hook. They had just fallen asleep. He answered barely looking at the screen. Ivy instantly grew angry, wondering who the fuck could be calling at this time of night on a Thursday. Jace heard faint cries and he knew something wasn't right. It was the same call he got when his brother was murdered months prior. He sat up straight, nervous to ask what was going on. But only this time it wasn't his mother on the other end, it was his Aunt Sharon crying. "They had to rush your mother to the hospital because she had a heart attack." Jace felt like he couldn't catch a break. First his brother and now his mother is laid up in some hospital without him. Ivy noticed how tense her man got and knew something was wrong. Losing his mother would crush him, especially after losing his brother. She knew firsthand what it felt like losing a parent. At that moment, she knew she would have to stand by her man because right now he would need her the most. He told his aunt he'd be on the first flight tomorrow afternoon. For the rest of the night he laid in Ivy's arms and they both cried together. Him reflecting on all the events that led up to this and her wishing she could have spoken to her mom before she found her dead.

Seated outside on 13th Street waiting for Ivy and Jamila to pull up, Nicole sat on her phone scrolling through Instagram as she waited for the duo. She noticed Vee had posted a video of her and some nigga. Her whole body got tense and she started to overheat. "So this nigga wants to play in my face huh? And this bitch thinks I'm a joke? Is this the reason this nigga disappeared off the face of the fuckin earth? So, this is the infamous Jace she's been ranting and raving about! Clearly he's feeding the bitch lies because Jace isn't even his real name, it's Jay! Ivy's always been naive when it comes to these niggas, man I tell you." Secretly deep down inside Nicole sat envious of Ivy's whole life. Whatever she wanted she got and Nicole always hated her for that...

"Girls, write three things you want for Christmas!" Mrs. Price said over breakfast one morning. Beaming with excitement, each girl abandoned their plates and ran off to scribble down exactly what they wanted to see under the Christmas tree. Nicole had fled the scene in search of a pen and pad. Weeks had

passed, and the big day was here. Some of the girls' wishes came true, while Nicole and a few others sat disappointed. This was the norm for a few of them so they brushed it off hoping that next year would finally be better for once. The following day, Nicole walked into Ivy's bedroom and noticed that her grandmother had got her the exact denim jean jacket that she prayed would be under her Christmas tree. She kept her composure in front of Ivy but later on she had a temper tantrum that caused a few of the girls to sleep downstairs for a few days. She cried herself to sleep that night yearning to just have a normal childhood where she got any and everything she wanted.

Slowly thinking back on when she first met Jay, she would fantasize about the perfect life they would have together. They'd be a married couple with children and a beautiful home with the white picket fence, success and good health... you know, the "American Dream". Nicole's dreams went to shit when she announced to Jay that he would be a daddy soon. It's like he did a whole 360 change and couldn't stand her guts. He made her abort the baby because he said he wasn't ready and jumped ship the night she got the abortion. It's like he vanished into thin air, leaving no trace of where he had gone. Nicole loved and cared about Jay so much that she wasn't herself for a few months after the abortion and seeing him hugged up with her best friend set the crazy switch upward. It was on now! Granted, Ivy never met Jay because their relationship was slightly hidden but she's seen pictures of him before. "Ivy knew he was my nigga first".

Nicole had been having it her way for some time now and at the rate she was going, it wouldn't be shocking if she became the first female president of the United States. She just basically got what she wanted out of life now. This wasn't the fifteen year old Nic that Ivy was use to dealing with. Revenge would be served how she likes her steaks, well done. With all that on her mind, Nicole didn't notice Ivy pull up in a burgundy Audi truck. She hopped out the passenger side and headed straight to her girlfriend. Nicole had butterflies. She slightly lowered her head so Jay couldn't see her. She then noticed Jamila walking up as well. Keeping her composure, Nicole shouted "bout fuckin time, I thought I was gone have to eat and drink alone, y'all hoes took forever" her heart was in her shoes she just couldn't believe it. She stayed calm and acted as normal as possible. An hour into their date, Nicole couldn't take it anymore and wanted to hear more about this infamous "Jace" character. "So Vee, tell us about your new little boo? The nigga you've been ditching us for, shit you even left Mik ass alone for this nigga!" "Yeah girl what he got a big dick?" Jamila blurted out and they all laughed.

"That's my Jacey boo, I love himmmmm" Ivy was smiling from ear to ear "he's everything" Nicole sat steaming on the inside.

Wishing that she had never even came looking for this bitch Ivy, Nicole sat hurting. After they were done eating, Ivy and Nicole headed to Target after they dropped Jamila off. Seated in the parking lot smoking a blunt, the girl's chit chatted about the latest shit going on in the world when Ivy's phone started to ring. Not recognizing the number she answered with much attitude "HELLO" the caller got straight to the point "shawty, I got my man Mik on the phone" Ivy's face turned cherry red. It's been literally six months since she had spoken to, seen or even wrote Mik. She had a change of heart about her and Mik being together while he was locked up. Being a ride or die bitch wasn't in her job description. Like how does that work? I don't even know if I'm coming or going so how in the hell am I gonna make sure his dumb ass is straight? She literally met Jace in a matter of weeks of Mik getting locked up and he knocked her socks off. Mik didn't stand a chance.

"Wassup baby" Mik said in his sweetest voice "Hey Mik Baby, wassup? Ivy was signaling Nicole to shut the hell up and get out of her face asking a million questions as if they were playing a game of charades. "BITCH", she thought she felt spit on her ear that's how hard he shouted through the phone "where the fuck you been? Why haven't I seen you? Matter fact, why the fuck

33

haven't you been answering my calls? I know you got all twenty five of my letters. I've been writing ya simple ass every day, bul got ya head fucked up huh?" Mik wouldn't let Ivy get a word in at all. "Like what type time you on Vee? You think it's cool to just up and disappear on a nigga and have me in here trying to put pieces of a fuckin puzzle together? Huh? That's wassup! I hope you have that same energy when I get home and trust me baby girl that's real soon. If I can't have you, can't nobody have you, bitch bet that" then the phone hung up.

"Oh my God, Ivy what did Mik say? Girl what he say? I know he's pissed with you! Chile, what you gonna do? Ignoring her, Ivy brushed that shit off and hopped out the car and headed into the store. Noticing that Ivy left her cellphone on the seat Nicole's plan for payback kicked in fast. "BINGO" Nicole reached over and grabbed the phone seated in her passenger seat. She went straight to Jace's name and picked up her own phone and started dialing the number as quickly as she could. She noticed Ivy walking back towards the car and threw the phone back in the seat trying her hardest to act natural. "This bitch looks like she's up to something" thought Ivy as she watched Nicole move uncontrollably in her seat. Let me make a mental note to keep my eye on this sneaky bitch because something isn't right with her. She's been doing the most lately. Getting back into the car she looked down at her phone and noticed she had a few missed calls from Jace. "Damn Nic, why you ain't answer and tell him I was in the store" side eyeing her now knowing something wasn't right. "'My bad Vee, I wasn't even thinking to answer" Nicole said nonchalantly. They pulled off silently and Ivy continued thinking of ways to get Mik out of her life and figure out what exactly her girlfriend was doing in the car.

Maxwell's "This Woman's Work" blasted through the speakers in the dimly lit house. The moonlight peeked through the closed curtains. Quietly sipping on her Riesling and taking small pulls of the blunt she had rolled, Ivy's mind had been on overdrive since she hung up the phone with Mik. Dates, times and locations kept coming to her but she had no idea why. Mik knew how to control her without him being in her presence. Yes she received all the threatening letters he had sent to her grandmother's house but that part of her life was over, so she thought. Jace had flown to Virginia to be with his sick mother for the week so now she was really on edge. "I hope this nigga doesn't come home on no bullshit! Why can't he just accept the fact that I finally moved on from his dumb ass?"

Chapter 7

Nicole hadn't slept well at all. Actually watching her best friend and man hugged up together fucked with her bad. She awoke this morning bleeding with envy and revenge on her mind. Ivy had to pay for not being loyal. The plan was to humiliate her in any way possible. Calling her up was on the agenda first. She wanted to spend as much time with Ivy before she destroyed her perfect little life. She had to get as much recent info as she could to throw back in Ivy's face later on. Nearly begging and pleading with this bitch for an hour, Ivy finally agreed to ride to New York with Nicole for the night. She kept complaining about Jace not wanting her in any clubs around any niggas and blah blah blah. The Jace I knew loved for his girl to have a good time. I wished this bitch would shut the fuck up, keep whining and complaining about what that nigga thinks. On their way they stopped and got a bottle of Hennessy for the road and to loosen Ivy's annoying ass up for the night she was about to have. The girls booked a room at the Marriott in Manhattan. Ivy, surprisingly in a better mood, wasted no time popping the top on the bottle of cognac. She had been in a state of depression since her man had flown down to Virginia and to make it worse she was receiving all kinds of horrible letters from Mik. "I'm going to make the best of my night, shit I'll deal with everything else tomorrow when I get back" she whispered as she downed the double shot she had just poured. Standing on the other side of the room, Nicole watched Ivy like a hawk. She noticed the sudden change in her attitude and a huge smile crept across her devious face. "This might be easier than I thought". Blasting 90's music, the girls continued getting dressed with their minds on two separate topics. Ivy was excited about all the fun the night would bring and Nicole was excited about how much of a disaster she was going to make Ivy's life. "Here girlfriend, drink some more, cause once we leave this room we won't be paying for anything else" Nicole boosted, handing over the drink. Drinking and putting the finishing touches on their makeup and outfits a sudden hard knock startled the girls. "Girl you ordered room service already?" Ivy said as she took the last bit of her drink pouring herself another. "Umm, it's my other dress I took it to laundry to have it steamed" Nicole replied casually. "What the fuck are they doing here this early? I told them midnight! It's only eleven fifteen; the bitch isn't even drunk yet!" Swinging the door open wide, there stood two big black Vin Diesel look alikes patiently waiting to be let in. Greeting both, Nicole introduced the two bodyguards as her homeboys from Brooklyn who was hanging out with them tonight. Noticing that the effects of the Xanax she had slipped into Ivy's drink earlier were taking its toll on her friend, she smiled happily. "GOT HER" Ivy always joking mumbled "What y'all gone do me like Junior did

Ebony? Laughing loudly showing that the alcohol and drugs were working.

Everything happened so quickly that Ivy didn't know what hit her when the shorter of the two guys hauled off and slapped her, immediately rushing and ripping off the dress she had on. Nicole quietly got out of their way and walked into the bathroom. Shutting the door and blasting the music up loud to drown out the cries for help from her best friend. She had a full blown conversation with some guy she just met the other night, while her two friends didn't come to play. They violated Ivy in more ways than one. Twenty minutes later Nicole emerged from the bathroom with a huge grin on her face. Her guys had got the job done and left minimum bruises so nothing would look out of place. She passed them an envelope with plans to meet up with them later on. Lightly walking over to Ivy's motionless body, she caressed her hair. Nicole leaned in whispering "Girl didn't ya momma ever tell you to watch people around your drinks?!"

The next morning Ivy opened her eyes and didn't recognize where she was. She had cotton mouth, along with a sore throat and a migraine. She looked to the left and noticed her girlfriend spread ass naked, knocked out beside her. Her adrenaline was on full blast. She panicked not being able to recollect last night's events. She hurried to the bathroom because her vagina and asshole felt like they were gonna fall off. Nothing was out of place but she did have a few stretches and small bruises on her arms and legs. Looking in the mirror she noticed red marks on her neck. "I need water, what the fuck did we get into last night?" This bitch has to get up and tell me every goddamn thing. Opening the bathroom door she noticed her dress balled up in the corner of the room. "Aye Nic, bitch get up! What did we do last night? I blacked out after that last shot you gave me" Clearly irritated and pissed off that Ivy's ass had woken up before she did. She hadn't come up with a bogus story to tell her. Going off the top of her head Nicole started laughing "Hoe never again am I inviting your embarrassing ass anywhere with me again!" Praying that this story seemed believable to get this dumb bitch out her face. "Girl, we didn't make it pass the hotel bar fucking with ya drunk ass. You wouldn't stop hollering about missing your precious boyfriend. You killed my whole vibe when you threw up on my damn $400 dress. I had to bring ya high ass back to the room" fake laughing "But I wasn't high last night" Ivy shot back " oh no, I meant drunk girl" Nicole started sweating thinking if this hoe don't lay the fuck off me with all the questions. "Hoe never again, you can't hang like you use to." Back in the car both girls were unusually quiet. Ivy thoughts were on her current problems and Nicole's on how to destroy this bitch faster because the sight of her made her sick.

Devastated that this wouldn't be the last time she'd see her, Nicole thought "I'm tired of this naive slut."

Chapter 8

It had been a few weeks and Jace still wasn't home. The last time she had seen him was when he dropped her off downtown and then headed straight to the airport. She understood that his mother was sick and he needed to be there with her to make sure she was okay, but shit what about me. This bastard wouldn't even allow me to fly down to see him. FaceTime, phone calls and text messages weren't enough at this point, she wanted her man home. Calling him up she decided to give him a piece of her mind. "When are you coming home?" Never the one to beat around the bush, Ivy knew she had to get right to the point. "Straight to the point, no hello or how you doing? Nothing huh?" He shot back irritated by her rudeness "Answer my question Jace!" She demanded. Jace thought it was cute when she got mad and missed him but he needed her to understand that she isn't his only priority. "Baby I told you I'm not sure yet, as soon as the doctors say my mom is doing okay, then I'll be on the first thing back to you! Get yah panties out yah ass I'll be there soon" he joked. Ivy felt like she accomplished nothing and just hung up the phone.

Clocking back in from lunch, Nicole had skipped all the way to her desk. While eating, she got a confirmation text telling her to check her email. Logging in she felt like she was opening a gift on Christmas morning. Excitement was written all over her face, she couldn't believe what she saw. She waited patiently for this and now she was ready to put her plan into motion. Lights, Camera, we've got fuckin Action ladies and gentlemen. Nicole slept like a baby that night.

Stepping into the humid air, Ivy's headache wasn't agreeing with the humid weather. A blunt and some Riesling were calling her name and she was on her way. Approaching her car, she noticed a male sitting on the hood. She couldn't tell who the man was because his back was towards her. "Excuse me, Can you..." the man turned around and smiled, stopping Ivy dead in her tracks. Jumping down off of the car and now face to face, Ivy's headache turned into a migraine that felt like it would never end. Passing over one single red rose and smiling from ear to ear, Mik knew he shocked the shit out of her. Mission Accomplished. Her whole face turned bright red showing her irritation level. "No hello Mikel? No hug? No kiss? Nothing huh?" Ivy wasn't scared of Mik at all but him popping up at her job spooked the shit out of her. She thought he was bullshitting when he said he'd be home sooner than later. "That's fucked up; I can't even get a welcome home baby or nothing? I swore we were better than that Vee" dropping his head he said in the gentlest tone "I missed you." Not speaking a word, she stepped pass him and headed to the driver's door and opened it. Not knowing what to say, Ivy just kept quiet in hopes that this would make him go away. Once upon a time, nobody not even Jesus himself could get her to turn her back on him. She felt herself turning around and running into his arms, but that chapter of her life was over, gone, and no longer in existence. Mik turned to walk away but then doubled back as if he still had a few things on his mind. "Remember what I told you last time we talked? Oh yeah. If I can't have you can't nobody can have you" he laughed as he walked away. He hopped into a pickup truck and sped off. Seated in the car Ivy's mind raced like a track meet. She just continued to ask herself "What the fuck am I going to do?

Chapter 9

Watching T.V., Jace was spread out on his mother's plush velvet sofa enjoying his time away from home. Nobody calling him with the bullshit was the best feeling there was. Only thing he missed was his beautiful girlfriend. He planned on proposing to her when he got back home. He felt she was the one for him and he hadn't felt that way about anybody ever before. She made him happy. He tried calling her but didn't get an answer. Probably running around with her girlfriends, he decided he'd get with her later. Just as he got up to go check on his mother, she walked into the den. He didn't like her on her feet but you can't stop a woman who's been on the go all her life so he chilled with lecturing her for now. She passed him a manila envelope marked urgent with his name on it from an address in Jersey. "Who the fuck is sending me shit down here? Nobody knows I'm down here." Ripping the envelope open he noticed there were photos and a letter. He automatically went to the letter trying to see who was sending him shit in Virginia.

Hey Jace,

I'm getting straight to the point. You don't know me but, I feel like you should know the things that have been going on while you're away. Your precious princess Ivy is a piece of dog shit. She's been cheating with several different men. That car she has was brought by a Chicago nigga right before she met you. That apartment she claimed she moved out of wasn't hers; it was her ex-boyfriends who she was living with. Oh yeah, she was just pregnant by him too. Also she was just in New York with some Brooklyn niggas. She's been super happy that you've been away for the past week and a half. Blah blah blah...

The rest of the letter was a blur. Jace was devastated and all he saw was red. He went through the envelope to see the other contents and almost shit his pants. There were pictures of Ivy ass naked with her mouth wrapped around some husky niggas dick, while another man had her bent over spreading her ass cheeks open. He only knew that was her because of the birthmark she had on her left cheek. It was more pictures but Jace couldn't stomach looking at the rest. "Fuckin bitch" I can't believe I fell for this scandalous ass whore. The news he just got started fucking with him mentally and his adrenaline was at an all-time high. He promised that he would not stop at any cost, until he got to the bottom of who sent the pictures and just what this smut bitch he intended to marry was really up to. His

45

mother watched from the door and knew something was about to go down and prayed that no one got hurt. "She's wants me home? Yeah I' ma meet the bitch there"

As much as it killed Nicole to invite Ivy over, she needed to see how she was holding up after their New York rendezvous. It fucked with Nicole that her only close friend would betray her like this. She wanted to cut all communication, but she needed this bitch around just to see her face when she and Jay showed her that they're back together. Hearing the knock at the door shook Nicole out of her twisted fantasies. Ivy walked in bearing a bottle of wine and some groceries. Realizing Nicole hadn't mentioned dinner, she decided to cook. Not even five minutes of her being in the apartment, the topic was switched to Jace. "I need to know if he told her about the pictures or not. But I should've known this bitch was gonna bring his ass up as soon as she got the opportunity" Nicole was over her company already. "Look, I didn't invite you over here to talk about ya stuck up ass boyfriend" Nicole barked. Ivy noticed the jealousy in her voice and vowed to never speak about him again because she sensed that she felt some type of way every time she brought his name up. "My bad sis" Ivy laughed it off. "Laugh now, but I'll have the last laugh when I have my man back sis" Nicole sneered as she finished her wine.

Rushing to get home to strangle this bitch, Jace took the first flight out of Richmond. He couldn't relax the whole flight; he didn't know what he was capable of doing once he saw Ivy. Every time he tried to fall asleep, imagines of her sucking another man's dick crushed him inside. He was drinking like a mad man on the plane and knocked everybody out of his way when the plane landed at the gate. He drove home as if stop signs and red lights didn't exist. Pulling up to their home, Jace couldn't stop the tears from falling. He was truly hurt by what he had seen earlier that day. Never in a million years would Ivy out of all people do this to him. How could she say she loved him when she did all this lying and cheating behind his back? She damn sure was going to pay. Creeping into the dark house he headed straight to their bedroom. Ivy was sound asleep without a care in the world. He thought about smothering her in her sleep but he needed her to know what the fuck she did wrong. Calming himself down, Jace decided he wasn't going act on this situation just yet. He was going to watch her every move and then when she least expected it, BOOM! He'll get her where it hurts just like this mystery person did to him. Sliding under the cover with her she instantly awoke. His face expression scared her and she instantly started crying because she felt that something was wrong due to the hurt in his eyes. He didn't speak a word; he just looked her in her eyes. Ivy didn't know what to say just that she was sorry. "Yeah bitch, I bet you are" Jace thought as he closed his eyes and held her until she fell back to sleep.

Chapter 10

Mik sat dipped in an old beat up 98 Honda Civic on the corner of Ivy's dark block. No one knew he was released from jail and he purposely did not disclose that information to anyone because folks ran their mouths too much. He asked around while he was in jail on her whereabouts and ended up with this address. Planning his every move was all he had been doing for the last few days. Trust and Loyalty is all he ever asked of Ivy and it's fucked up that he had to find out certain shit from random niggas. "If she knew she didn't wanna be with a nigga no more, why not just say that? Don't just cut me the fuck off like I'm some flea" he said to himself. Waiting patiently to make his move he noticed a burgundy truck pull up in front of the house. A tall basketball player looking nigga emerged and headed towards the front door. "So Jace is the nigga she's been dealing with" immediately he identified the tall slender dude. "Stinking bitch" he spat as he had flashbacks of her standing at the front door half naked waiting for him to come in for the night, or how she'd be on his line cursing him out about a bitch calling her phone saying they were together. Man just the overall love she had for a nigga. Then he started thinking about all of the letters he read and all the conversations he had while he was locked up, basically saying "'you lost yah girl". His blood boiled with envy, and hurt. "She's going to pay for this shit" he sat up straight and pulled off; she's not getting away with none of this...

A group of men stood on the court smoking, drinking, gambling and just shit talking. Mik stood out because he was always the loudest so Jay had no problem spotting him. Walking up to the dice game, Jay wasted no time letting his presence be felt. "You a day late and a dollar short cuz, don't you owe me some bread? How you out here gambling but you owe me my shit? And you losing? Jay firmly stood in front of Mik. Mik had been scheming since day one and never once thought Jay would realize. Jace had warned his brother not to fuck with this nigga because he was a petty malicious motherfucker. Robbing his own mother was in his DNA so burning Jay for a couple thousands wasn't a surprise. Refusing to listen to his brothers words, Jay fucked with Mik not realizing that this nigga just ain't give a fuck about nothing. Continuously trying to finesse his way out of this, Mik knew Jay wasn't buying the bullshit. Jay gripped him up against the fence that outlined the basketball court with one hand and swiftly pulled his gun out with the other placing the steel under Mik's bearded chin. "I want my money by the end of the week cuz or we gone have a major problem" Jay had blood in his eyes. This only caused Mik to swell up with anger. Releasing him, Jay secured his gun back in the lining of his coat and told Mik to get with him. Walking off with all eyes on him, Jay walked back to his car. "Aye Jay" Mik shouted "next time you pull a gun out, you better use it pussy" Mik let off two clean shots, one in his chest and the other through his eyes.

Ivy awoke to an empty bed. She had the most peaceful dream last night and it felt so real. She dreamt that her man had finally come home and made passionate love to her but that clearly was a dream because his side of the bed was still cold. Noticing his clothes scattered around their room, he had actually been there. Getting up to get her day started she checked her cellphone and there was two messages, one was from Jace. She read the message and an instant attitude came after. "I didn't want to wake you, you were sleeping so peaceful! I'll call you later when I get sometime"... The fuck he mean when he gets some time? Dialing his number she got so heated because her calls kept going to voicemail. So she wasn't dreaming, her man was back but obviously he was on some nut shit this time around. Overly irritated, Ivy didn't even bother to check her other message. Calling over and over and still getting nothing but his answering machine, Ivy got up and started her day. "Fuck him since he wanna come home on his best bullshit, I haven't done shit to that pussy so let him stay mad for whatever reason"

Chapter 11

The DJ was lit. The crowd was a good vibe and the playas were buying bottles left and right. Jamila and Nicole were looking like money as usual and had everyone's attention. Seated in the clubs back section, they danced and drank like it was going out of style. Jamila noticed a girl from around the way named Reese, making her way towards their section. She was a known whore who loved to stir the pot for unwanted drama and tonight was no different. "Hey y'all, wassup?" Jamila gave a fake hello but surprisingly Nicole welcomes this hoe with open arms giving her the biggest hug. A few seconds of small talk and then Reese wasted no time "Where's Ivy?" Nicole's whole mood changed dramatically and that's when the drunken tongue started speaking the sober truth. "Fuck that snake ass Bitch!" She wasn't loyal; all she cares about is that nigga, FUCK HERRR." eyes wide open, Jamila and a few of the guys they were partying with couldn't believe the shade Nic had just thrown at Ivy and Reese was the sponge, sitting there soaking it all up. Instantly Jamila knew something had to be up, but what? Grabbing the Henny bottle out of Nicole's hand, Jamila said her goodbyes and dragged Nicole's drunk ass out of the club doors. "Bitch what was that all about huh?" Jamila spat as soon as they were getting into the car. Nicole never realized that she threw her own best friend under the bus to Reese, Channel 10. Letting everything on her mind flow, Nicole let it all out. "I hate Vee man; she took, took the one person who I ever loved. The one person who finally loved me back, the one I was suppose to have a child with. This is the reason she never brought him around because she knew, she knew my feelings for him. I'm going to ruin her watch" Now Jamila is completely unaware of what the hell Nicole was rambling about because her speech was half slurred but quickly made a mental note to pick Ivy's brain real soon because some shit just wasn't adding up. Finally, calming her friend down, she pulled off and drove her home.

Across the city Mik tried erasing Ivy from his mental but it was hard. Everything reminded him of her. Seeing women with red lipstick made him aggy because that was her signature color. When The Notebook came on television, he changed the channel because that was her favorite movie. He wanted to curse out the "Kelly Bundy" Dumbo seated across from him because she ordered her martini just like Ivy did. His mind couldn't escape her even if he wanted to. He tried to even deal with other women but none of them seemed to match her. Either they were pretty with no personality or just plain ugly and hype to be in his presence. In reality, Mik would give up his whole life to be with Ivy; he worshipped everything about her. Frustration covered his face and Kelly Bundy wished she hadn't asked him what was wrong. "Does it look like something's wrong" he fired back completely shocking the innocent girl "Matter fact get ya shit, we out! Naw! Matter fact, you find your own way home" dropping money on the table for the bill, he grabbed his coat and left the restaurant. Putting his hand around Ivy's neck was the only thing on his mind.

 Waking up with a dry mouth and Jay on her mind, Nicole decided that today would be the day she got her man back. "FUCK IVY" she had a text free number that she used just in case her planned backfired, nobody had a way of tracing it back to her real number. She told him that she had some news that may interest him and he bit the apple faster than Eve did. Agreeing to meet her in a few hours, Nicole wrecked her brain on what outfit she could wear. "I'm going all out, he needs to see what he left alone" as she ran her bath water she started reminiscing. Never in her right state of mind would she have ever thought of him leaving her how he did. He never introduced her to any of his family or friends so contacting any of them were distant thoughts. Basically she was stuck in park while he was switching lanes in life. "Get ya life together sis, you about to get ya man back, so save all that extra emotional shit for something else" As she sat in the hot steamy water , she envisioned Jay coming home with her tonight and caressing every inch of her broken soul. She yearned for his touch, fuck that she craved for him.

Chapter 12

"Can we meet? I have a few things that may interest you? Jace frowned not recognizing the number. He then realized that this may be the same person who had sent him the photos to his mom's house. Receiving the random text set all types of alarms off in Jace's mind. He got frustrated quick, it had to be a person that was close to him because this was his personal phone number. Also nobody knew he was even away besides Ivy, his mom and Aunt Sharon. Something fishy was going on and he planned to find out where that smell was coming from. "Yeah we can meet at Davio's on 17th street in two hours" Jace said quickly. Always the type of guy to be on time, Jace headed in the direction of the restaurant disregarding any of the business he had to handle that day. Finding out who this mystery person was killing him and it was his top priority at this point. He needed to know who and why this person was so pressed to share all this information with him. Pulling up and scoring a good parking spot diagonally across from the restaurant, Jace sat in his beat up Ford Taurus. He wouldn't be dead caught in his truck. Knowing that whoever it was probably knew exactly what he drove so he had to think smart. Being dumb didn't get him this far in life so he sat silently, plotting as he watched out for familiar faces in the crowd of people strolling by.

Sitting there waiting for this mystery person for twenty minutes had Jace on edge and seemed to be forever. Getting that gut feeling he always got when he knew something wasn't right started eating at him. "Something isn't right, I can feel that shit" just as those words left Jace's mouth his scandalous ass girlfriends car pulls up directly in front of the restaurant. "What the fuck is she doing down here? She just told me she wasn't feeling good and she was lying down. If a nigga hops out of this fucking car they're both gonna regret they didn't pick another restaurant." Jace leaned under his seat for his gun when he heard a text message ring out. "I'm here" As he looked back up he noticed the passenger door swing open and he went for his door handle. He stopped in his tracks as he noticed the person getting out of the car. "Nicole" he whispered as if someone could hear him. Quickly he responded "be there in 5" to the message as fast as he could. Squinting his eyes he noticed Nicole look at her phone and smile. Confusion was written all over his face. "What the fuck is going on? For the first time in life he didn't know what to do or what to say. "But why? What's her whole thing? She's Ivy's best friend, so why would she give up tape on her? I never even met this girl, so what the fuck?" A bunch of why's crept up in his mind. If he was confused before well now he's lost and couldn't wrap his head around what this bitch was up to. Ivy pulled off and Jace sat puzzled. "Should I go in? Or should I leave?" Playing around with his decision, Jace put his gun back under his seat and got out the car. Curiosity was getting the best of him. "What was this all about? I hope this bitch not tryna line me or Ima kill her" he thought twice and pulled his gun back out.

Creeping back up the block slowly, Ivy looked out to see if she peeped any friendly faces since Nic didn't wanna give up who she was meeting. As if she was fucking the president and didn't want the first lady to find out. Not missing a beat, Ivy noticed her own nigga walking quickly to the front door of the restaurant. "That pussy just told me he was in Jersey, how the fuck is he walking his big headed ass six feet away from my car?" Slowing the car down so that he wasn't able to notice her presence, the thought of running him over crossed her mind. Red with fury, Ivy drilled her fist into the steering wheel. "This the reason this bitch didn't want me dropping her off at the front door and wouldn't tell me who she was meeting? Then this dickhead kept calling me asking me what the fuck I was doing to make sure I was nowhere near here. Well guess what motherfucker, I'M HERE!" Ivy screamed "I couldn't believe this bullshit; he's fucking my best friend?" Tears entered the corner of her eyes and started rolling down her cheeks. Pulling off just as quickly as she came she promised on her mother's grave somebody was going to pay.

Walking into the restaurant Jace was spooked. He didn't know what he was walking into but he was strapped so his chances of getting out alive were possible. He saw Nicole sitting at the bar patiently waiting. Never ever meeting this girl a day in his life, he only had seen her in pictures and through conversation so he's still mind blown at why she was so persistent with meeting him. He needed to see what the fuck she had to say out of those pretty lips of hers.

"Nicole right? Jace said as he extended his hand to shake hers. Nice to finally meet you, heard nothing but great things. Jace was using everything in his power not to pull his gun out on this sneaky bitch and ask her what her motive was. Since his brother got killed, Jace's patience was paper thin and he didn't deal with any nonsense whatsoever so he's giving this bitch a pass like he's been giving Ivy's trifling ass. Instead he killed her with kindness because he knew she was thinking he was going to approach her all defensive. Before speaking, Nicole ordered crab cakes and a glass of Merlot while ordering him a double shot of Hennessy. In her soul, she was hurt that he didn't acknowledge her. No nice to see you Nicole, NOTHING! She was extremely hurt but acted as if this was her first time ever meeting him. Two can play this game. "I've heard nothing but awesome things about you as well Mr. Jace, too bad we had to meet under these circumstances". Toying around with her thoughts, Nicole couldn't bring herself to just come out and air Ivy's fake business because she was memorized by Jace. Everything about him was perfect, literally. His teeth, smile, his complexion, everything. Wanting to pull his dick out and suck it in the middle of the restaurant crossed her mind more than once while looking him in his eyes. Snapping out of her daydream, she got straight to why they were there.

"Ivy is my girl and I love her to death but the way she's been carrying you since day one is fucked up" taking a sip of her wine she watched as his half smile disappeared into a frown, his jaw tighten and he moved uncomfortably in his seat. "GOT HIM". "I couldn't continue to take her calling me day in and day out about whom she's been fucking while you were away in Virginia, taking care of your sick mother. Saying shit like "what he doesn't know won't kill him" Nicole giggled inside because of all the bullshit she was feeding him and this nigga was eating it all up. She only knew he was in VA because she overheard Ivy speaking to him about being away one night, but then the sadness came over her because he still hadn't acknowledge her and clearly he was more in love with this bitch Ivy. Admitting to sending the pictures and letters Nicole tried to get through to Jace but he seemed to vanish to a faraway place as they were seated at the bar. He quickly got up, gave her some money for the bill and left.

Chapter 13

Disgusted at the way their date went, Nicole felt like she accomplished nothing. Jace was clearly still madly in love with his precious Ivy. "What did she have that I didn't?" seated in the back seat of the Uber, Nicole's body lit up with rage. She tried to take her mind off of the fact that she still didn't get her man back. "Well I didn't think he was going to grab my hand and we would walk off into the sunset together but damn we did have this little perfect life at one point in time" Hopping out of the car she rushed into her apartment trying to hold back the tears. Ending up in the bathroom, she watched her reflection in the mirror. She noticed the younger Nicole crying. Looking closely, she realized that was the last day she saw her mother...

"Baby girl, I promise I'll be back tomorrow" Karen said cupping her daughter's chubby cheeks in her hands. "This place is real nice Nic; I heard they got lots of toys and all the cartoon movies you like to watch. They even have all the popcorn and ice cream you can eat baby. I'll be back first thing in the morning so be ready" Giving her only child a kiss she saw the tears forming in her eyes. Nicole's face was full of tears, stepping back into the house she watched her mother scurry up the block. That was Nicole's last time seeing Karen alive. Some years had passed and her foster mother, Mrs. Price came into her room to give her the

awful news. Her mother had died of AIDS a few days ago. Nicole
didn't feel any pain; no remorse, she didn't even shed a tear.
How could she? She didn't know that lady. In her world her
mother died that morning she didn't show up to take her home.
Concerned with Nicole's emotionless attitude and quick temper,
Mrs. Price took her to see a specialist. At the time Nicole was
only ten years old and felt the whole process was bullshit. The
specialist diagnosed Nicole with Reactive Attachment Disorder.
Explaining to Mrs. Price that this disorder is defined as a
condition in which individuals have difficulty forming lasting
relationships. Detached and unresponsive behavior usually
develops as a child. Most children with attachment disorder
have severe problems or difficulties in early relationships. All in
all, being neglected by a parent such as the mother, a child
doesn't develop an attachment to the rest of the world.
Everything made sense to Mrs. Price now but there was nothing
she could do. Nicole was a fucked up child and she prayed this
all was a phase and by the time she reached adulthood it would
be over, hopefully.

Seeing her eyes blood red, Nicole tried to piece herself
together. She was angry that she allowed herself to think of her
mother. She became furious for allowing herself to love Jay. On
that morning that her mother didn't show up, she vowed to
never love anyone as hard as she loved her mom. Never to

depend on anybody and never let them see you cry. Slamming her fist into the mirror it instantly broke. Breaking down she hated Jay for leaving her like her mom did. He made her get rid of the only person who may have possibly loved her back, her baby, she aborted for him. She slid to the floor and cried for her unborn child.

"I should've left my baby girl a message" Mik sang along with Donell Jones as he rode around with no destination. The humidity was high and Mik was even higher. Washing down two Percocet 15's with a half pint of Remy Martin, Mik sat in a daze. His emotions were on overdrive and he didn't know what he was capable of doing at this point. His heart was crushed because the woman he loved so much didn't love him back. Trying his hardest to leave her in his past, an image of her always came back to haunt his dreams. Drinking and popping pills were his only escape but he still couldn't shake his "Ivy Blues". Riding in the crisp air, Mik ended up parked outside of Ivy and Jace's house. The Remy gave him all the courage he needed. Not giving a flying fuck if Ivy was with this clown, he needed to see her and let her know how he felt. After sitting for ten minutes, Mik grew overly impatient because there were no traces of Ivy popping up any time soon. Getting out of the car the hot air hit his face, Mik grew more agitated. Walking towards the porch he noticed two chairs to the far left and stumbled his way to one. "This nigga better not be with her or it's on" he casually talked as if he had an audience.

Pulling up with the weight of the world on her shoulders, Ivy never noticed she had company. Never in a zillion years would she believe the two most important people in her life would cross her. Never taking her mind off the bullshit she searched around for her house keys. "I taught you better than this? Since you shacked up here with this nigga you forgot to watch your surroundings?" Mik set straight up in the chair observing her lack of judgement. Ivy pissed her pants literally. Jace had her mind fucked up and had her losing focus. "Mik, what the fuck are you doing on my goddamn porch? Nigga how the fuck do you know where I live? I let that shit you did at my job slide but you outta order showing the fuck up at my house! The fuck is wrong with you? Why can't you accept that I've moved on from ya trifling ass. I got a new nigga and you're lucky he isn't with me to handle ya high dumbass. Now get the fuck off my porch!" Ivy was heated and was ready for war. In a quick second she ain't know what hit her. Mik hauled off and punched her dead in her nose. Blood was all over her face as he gripped her by her neck forcing her in the house. Holding both of her arms down by her wrist on her white leather couch, Ivy squirmed her legs trying to get him off of her. "You think that nigga better than me? You think he gives a fuck about you?" Mik screamed. Ivy didn't cry up until he said those words. She kept having visions of Jace fucking Nicole and she just kept smiling back at her. Breaking her out of her daydream, Mik smacked Ivy so hard the sting felt worse than the slap. "I ain't do shit but love you" as he loosened his grip on her wrist, he wiped her tears away. The tears didn't mean shit to him though. Picking her petite body off of the couch he slammed her onto their glass coffee table. Grabbing her neck once again, Mik tighten his grip. Laughing to himself he muttered "this bitch got me fucked up" this was her last time disrespecting him...

"Mik, baby please go to your room! Mommy is ok. Daddy just wants to talk to me about some things" dragging his feet all the way to his room, Mik didn't wanna leave his mother alone ever again. He knew what might happen if he did. Like clockwork, Rebecca's faint cries could be heard as Mark beat his wife til he turned purple in the face. Continuously, Mikel watched his father beat his mother like she stole from him. He always wondered and asked his mother why his father was so angry at her all the time. Rebecca would make some bullshit lie up about him being stressed and she didn't help with all her wants and needs every minute of the day. Mik vowed to never hit a woman like his father beat his mother.

In that instant moment, Mik looked at himself in the mirror and saw his father. Tears welled up in his eyes and he couldn't believe he had turned into his father. But there was no turning back, Ivy deserved this. Finally calming himself down, Mik pulled Ivy's tear filled face to his. She could smell the alcohol on his breath. "This shit still aint over" he kissed her swollen lips and walked out the door as if nothing ever happened. Sobbing uncontrollably, Ivy didn't even bother to move. She laid in the middle of her living room floor asking God to send her some strength cause at this time she needed it the most. Jace didn't come home that night and she was kind of relieved because she didn't want to face him like this. She knew every word Mik spat had the truth behind it. Explaining all of what happened would've been hard considering she didn't even have all the answers herself. With a migraine out of this world, Ivy managed to gain some strength and clean up the Disaster Hurricane Mik has caused. Running a hot shower, Ivy mixed the water with her tears knowing everything would get worse before they got better.

Chapter 14

Jace's head was all fucked up. He felt everybody was shady now and couldn't trust a soul. He knew Nicole had some underlying information but wouldn't let him in on it. Her way was to expose Ivy's trifling ass first and then pop up with some more shit. Sneaky bitches. Deciding to stay at a nearby hotel, Jace couldn't stand to see the sight of Ivy right now.

Mik felt no remorse for what he'd done to Ivy. The bitch deserved it, she's lucky I don't kill her ass. She left me when I was down for a nigga who doesn't even care about her. Mik was high once again and didn't care about anything or anyone.

Not being able to get this man off her mind, Nicole pulled herself together and headed to Delaware to pay someone a visit. She had only been to their house a handful of times but knew every detail as if she built it her damn self. She even knew how many houses down from the corner it was. Nicole needed Jace to explain to her why he just left her high and dry. Pulling up, she glanced and noticed Ivy's Benz parked out front. Instantly aggravated, she didn't give a fuck at this point. She needed answers and she was gonna get them voluntarily or she was gonna invite herself in involuntarily. No sight of his truck so she waited in her raggedy ass Altima. Watching a few neighbors come and go, nothing out of the ordinary until the front door swung open. Mik came walking out as if this was his fuckin crib. "When the fuck did he come home and why the fuck is he leaving out of their house? Oh see this is the shit I'm talking about, this hoe ain't right. But this is the bitch who he wants to be with? DUMB ASS!" Quietly snapping pictures, Nicole couldn't wait to expose her "bestie" as tears welled up in her eyes.

Jamila needed to get away from her two bad ass kids and annoying baby father. She hadn't spoken to her girls all week and decided to see if they were down to grab a few drinks. Ivy declined saying she had shit to do for work and Nicole didn't answer. She still lived in the hood so running into somebody she knew to kick it with for the night wouldn't be hard, so she headed to the bar around the corner to get her night started. Ordering a Long Island, she didn't notice any familiar faces until she laid eyes on Reese. Annoyed and trying to cover her face, Reese had already peeped Jamila and decided to stroll on back to where she was seated at the bar. "Hey boo", Reese said all loud and excited as if they've been friends all their lives. Giving her a dry hello like always Jamila rose from her seat. "Girl I ain't that damn bad sit down and finish ya drink" Reese said with an attitude. Jamila sat back down taking a long pull at her straw. Moments had passed before any of the two spoke. "Where Nic and Ivy at?" Reese said breaking the silence. "They still beefing over that nigga I see." "Loud mouth bitch" Jamila thought to herself as she turned her nose up. The way she said it was as if she had more tea on what was going on between the duo. Jamila gave Reese the dirtiest look, but Reese so caught up in the gossip, didn't notice it. The double shot of Patron Reese had was taking effect and her mouth started going. "My cousin Kim had peeped Jace and Nic in Davio's the other night looking real fuckin acquainted" Jamila sat stunned at what she had just heard but she didn't give Reese any emotion. "Girl Mik was talking real heavy too about Jace and his brother Jay. How he got Jay outta here and Jace knows and won't do shit about it" flagging down the bartender Jamila said fuck the drink and ordered two double shots of Henny and told the big butt bartender to keep them coming. The news had shocked the shit out of her and she couldn't believe this was all going down under her nose. Soaking up everything Reese just said she made a mental note to see what else had been being said out here. The shade Nicole threw at Ivy at the club wasn't for nothing. Mik just up and getting locked up a few months ago now made sense and why Ivy had been being real distant. It's all making sense now. But does everyone know about what's going down? Like does Ivy know her best friend could possibly be fucking her man? Did Jace really know Mik killed his brother? Did Nicole know she was seen with Jace? Shit just keeps on getting weirder and weirder. "You run ya mouth too much Reese" slurred Jamila clearly letting the liquor take over her body. "So I've been told" Reese shot back rubbing Jamila's leg. Reese never seemed to be the type that was attracted to women, but Jamila didn't seem to mind considering she low key had a crush on Reese for years. One would assume that was the reason Jamila was so bothered by her presence every time she came around; she secretly wanted her. Reese wasn't the best looking duck in the pond but it was something about her confidence that lit Jamila's fire. The effect of the alcohol had them both feeling super good and real kinky. Reese grabbed Jamila's hands and led her out of the bar. Jamila suggested they take the rest of the party to Reese's house because her house was occupied with bad ass kids and a worthless baby father.

Arriving to a row house about fifteen minutes away, Jamila was shocked to see that Reese had a decent home. She always gave her dirty whore jawn who used sheets for curtains and had every roach in the city creeping and crawling around her house. She was impressed. Lighting a blunt and passing it, Reese could see the nervousness on Jamila's face and tried to soften the mood. Taking a few pulls, Jamila was instantly in the mood and walked over to Reese as she sat on her couch. Kissing and touching both women grew excited, not believing that this was really happening. A more experienced Reese took control and led Jamila upstairs towards her bedroom. Slowing undressing each other they didn't make a sound. Just passionate kisses and dreamy eyes as they caressed one another. Laying Jamila down on her back, Reese started with her lips and headed straight down. Craving this perfect touch for so long, Jamila couldn't hold in her moans. "BANG BANG" the hard knock on the front door startled both women outta their pure bliss. Reese tried to ignore the pounding in hopes that whoever was interrupting her would just go away. Jamila tensed up and Reese became agitated, racing towards the door to give whoever it was a piece of her mind.

Chapter 15

Curiosity killed the cat. Jace didn't walk through the door that night and the wine mixed with weed got the best of Ivy's feelings. His iPad sat on the nightstand and it was linked to his phone. She wanted to see if he was dealing with any other women she should know about. She tried her luck with his password. Typing his mother's birthday the phone came alive. Going directly to his photos there was nothing but pictures of them. She then went through text messages and still came up short. Her good conscience said " girl your man is faithful, he only loves you" but her devilish conscience put the battery in her back to continue snooping until she found something which lead her straight to the emails. Scrolling through, she noticed nothing out of the ordinary. Basic shit like promotional codes for department stores, airline deals and renewal emails for the local gym. But that's when she noticed an email from someone named Smith, with the subject reading "Sent them via Email too". Clicking on the email she went straight to the attachments and at that moment Ivy lost all motion in her body as she saw images of herself butt ass naked in a hotel room with a dick in her mouth and another in her ass. She couldn't believe it. She scrolled down further and saw a picture of Mik coming out of her home, instantly realizing that these photos were taken within the last month. Slowly passing all of the horrible pictures, Ivy went to see the email address which only read smith00@gmail.com. Mentally storing the address in her memory she logged out of the iPad and with tears in her eyes she slid into her bed. Who would possibly want to destroy me this bad? "Who the fuck was those men? And what exactly is Jace thinking and why hasn't he brought this to my attention yet because it's clear that he opened the email already so he knows. I know he's been looking at me in disgust. What could I possibly say or do to make him believe me?" Crying herself silently to sleep she promised she'd crack this case as if she worked for SVU.

Chapter 16

Halfway to the door you would've thought the door was off the hinges already. "Motherfucker is you crazy?" Reese screamed finally making it to the door. She could already see what type of night she was about to have. Mik had been drinking and she didn't want to do or say anything that might tick him off. "Why you aint got no fuckin clothes on?" Mik scanned the room. Praying silently that Jamila kept her ass upstairs, Reese thought quick on her feet. "I was about to shower then you came banging on my goddamn door. Slowly walking towards her Mik liked what he saw. She aint have shit on Ivy but she could get the job done for now. Frustrated that he was here and messing up her groove, she thought the quicker the better. Lowering her body until she was on her knees, she unfastened his belt and pulled down his jeans. Putting every inch of his swollen penis into her tiny mouth till it disappeared. Jamila tiptoed to the top of the steps to connect the face to the voice she heard from the bedroom. Reese had never been the type to have one steady nigga so Jamila knew it was some random guy at her door coming to get his shit off. Peaking downstairs, she watched as Reese sucked the skin off of Mik's dick. She was completely surprised that Mik would even deal with this loud mouth bitch but then her thoughts confused her because she was just about to be fucked by this same loud mouth bitch. "How the fuck am I gonna get out of here? And how the fuck am I gonna tell Nic and Ivy?" Getting dressed, Jamila tried to figure out ways to get out of Reese's house without being seen but her car keys were on the living room table so it seemed like she would be stuck for a while. Being held hostage, an hour had passed and Jamila was irritated. "Bul left yet?" getting straight to the point. "He passed out, he'll be gone for the rest of the night" Reese said proudly. Walking pass Reese, Jamila headed to the front door. With plans to see her again, she turned and told Reese to put her number in her phone with hopes that she would have some more tea like she did tonight. In the car, she sat trying to wrap her head around everything she had just heard and seen tonight. Ivy had to be the first person she called in the morning.

Soundlessly sitting in the cold room waiting nervously for the doctor, Ivy tried her hardest to hold back the tears. Why me Lord? What have I done to deserve half of this pain? I never crossed a soul in my life. Is it Karma for leaving Mik while he was in jail? What the fuck is it? Tears released themselves onto the paper thin gown. The images were still so clear in her mind that she couldn't shake the thoughts. Several things crossed her mind as she had flashbacks of her mother. She doesn't recall having sex with those guys in the pictures so what if she contracted some sort of STD or even worst AIDS like her

mother. Interrupting Ivy's thoughts Dr. Patel knocked on the
door and welcomed herself in. The doctor instantly noticed the
tears in Ivy's eyes, however assuming she was nervous she
decided against questioning her. "Okay, Mrs. Smith your pap
smear was normal and all test came back negative but I'm afraid
I have some other news for you" Dr. Patel said with a straight
face. "Omg I have HIV don't I doctor? This is horrible. How am I
going to explain this to Jace he already hates me? Why me
doctor?" Ivy would not stop crying as a confused Dr. Patel sat
staring at her emotionless. "Umm Ivy, no sweetheart you don't
have HIV, you're pregnant" Crying even more Ivy shouted "I
gave my baby HIV, oh no Lord why?" Dr. Patel didn't know what
to do at this point. Trying to calm the dramatic young lady
down, she had to explain herself one more time. "Ivy, you have
not contracted the Aids Virus. You're a healthy woman with
hopes of delivering a healthy baby."

Settling down listening to what the doctor had to say, Ivy
released a deep breath. Finally registering all that had just
happened she now wore a huge smile on her face. A smile that
almost immediately turned into a frown once the possibility
that this may not be Jace's baby that's she carrying crossed her
mind. Continuously apologizing to Dr. Patel, Ivy took her things
and hurried off. On the drive home she envisioned what her

unborn child would look like; just praying that Jace was the father.

Jace sat in his truck smoking a blunt piecing together his life. In the last seven months, a lot of bullshit had transpired. He just wanted to get to the bottom of all this nonsense and get on with his life. Getting a call from his man Dee snapped him out of his daydream. Jace hoped Dee wasn't calling him to talk about any dumb shit, but that was too good to be true. "Shit getting goofy outchea man" Dee talked as he dragged his words. "Naw shit been goofy outchea. I've been hearing some foul shit from out of a couple niggas mouth" Unbothered by what Dee was saying, Jace just kept smoking and half listening. "Not the one to be the bearer of bad news fam but I wouldn't be ya man if I ain't speak on this shit" Now Jace's antennas were up. He wished Dee would just stop talking and say what was on his mind. "Man the streets been talking and" Jace now annoyed "Nigga speak the fuck up, this aint no guessing game. What you been hearing?" Dee got real quiet and then just blurted it out. "They saying Mik killed Jay man and you knew about it and aint did or gone do shit" Jace whole body turned hot...

Jay called Jace yelling. "Bro calm down, what the fuck happened? Jay continued to yell "Bro come scoop me NOW!" Getting his location, Jace wasted no time. Speeding to the destination, he arrived at a subdivision in Cherry Hill, New

Jersey. The sun was setting and Jace had no clue what the fuck was going on. Calling Jay to let him know he was there, Jay told him to come to a particular spot. Following directions to a T, Jace was looking through all his mirrors to see if he saw anything. Two minutes later, he saw his brother and this bum ass nigga Mik emerge from under two parked cars. As Jay and Mik got into the car in a hurry Jace instantly put the car into drive and pulled off before they could even shut the doors. "What type time you on Bro?" Jace asked calmly. "Man, I don't even wanna talk about this shit" Jay sat staring out the window. Dropping the conversation, Jace glanced in his rear view mirror and looked Mik dead in his eyes. "This nigga has got to go". Jace kept a mental note to keep his eyes on this sneaky nigga. "Man I told you not to fuck with that nigga, he's shady bro" Jace sat telling his hard headed ass brother. "He'll do anything for a dollar, a nigga like that you can't trust yo" Jay brushed off what his brother was saying. He was just being protective Jace like always. "Bro I got this, that nigga know not to play with me, trust! Jay hugged his big brother and drove off.

Repeating their last conversation over and over, Jace grew madder and madder. This nigga Mik was going to see just what he was capable of. Jace and Jay had not grown up in Philly, they were from Camden. The brother's grandmother lived here so they learned their way around the streets during summer and holiday visits. Jay decided to dwindle in the street life while Jace took the back seat and started running small businesses. Both brothers were very successful in their endeavors but in both their minds they wanted more. Over the years, they would meet all kinds of people, the good, bad and the fucking ugly. Jace was the older of the two and with him being the big brother he always protected his baby bro no matter what. Jace wasn't a street nigga by a long shot but when it came to his brother; oh he most definitely was going to put up a fight to handle shit.

Chapter 17

Opening my eyes slightly, the sun peeped through the curtains confirming that he had showed up to do his shift for the day. Narrowing in on the clock, it wasn't time for me to get up but the faint kisses on my neck told me otherwise. I knew a certain someone was ready to get his day started. As he ran that thick tongue from my neck to my shoulders and then down until he reached my erect nipples, I let out a soft moan. Giving him confirmation that I was fully awake now, he continued to slide that juicy tongue lower and lower, I looked up to get a clearer view. I always enjoyed watching. "Make it messy" I moaned out while reaching to caress my puffy nipples as he sent an electric shock through my ass. The way he spat and nibbled on my clit was like no other and it caused my body to be so sensitive that every touch turned me on. Grabbing his face giving him a long deep kiss, he slid that colossal penis inside me and I released the biggest moan; I could've woke my neighbors. Whispering his name turned him on and he picked up his pace. Through our heavy breathing a small distant vibrating noise could be heard coming from across the room. It would start up and then stop and then start buzzing again. Growing tired of the overly active phone, I pushed him. "Just answer your damn phone"

"Ugggghh" screamed a frustrated Jace , knowing that whoever

it was fucked up his chances of getting off because he was pretty sure she wasn't going to be up to finish what they started after he got up to check the phone. Jace had decided to sneak back into the house after being gone for several days. He came in while Ivy was sleep because he didn't want to hear her mouth about where he had been, but he grew tired of sleeping in hotel beds and honestly, although hard to admit, he missed Ivy.

Nicole was at the free throw line in the fourth quarter with five seconds on the clock and needed these points like her life depended on them. Actually it did. She needed Jay or whatever the hell he called himself nowadays to come to the realization that she's been about him since day one. Their lives could and would be so much better. Losing one of her closest friends did not bother her one bit at this point. She wanted her man back.

Cursing under her breath, Ivy got up to take a shower since her picnic got rained on. Stepping into the steamy shower, Ivy was low key excited that her man had finally stopped punishing her and had come home. Then the pictures popped in her head. Lowering her head she released tears hoping he'd come join her. Her juices started flowing when she heard the bathroom door crack. Pulling the shower curtain back at full speed, Ivy couldn't read the expression spread across his face, but it was one she hadn't seen before. He was fully clothed and you could see the steam coming out of his ears. "Bitch you fucked that nigga in my house?" Instantly knowing that he was referring to Mik. "Baby, NO I would never!" Shoving his phone into her face, there were a nice amount of pictures of Mik, clearly walking out of their front door. Staring in shock, Ivy opened her mouth but nothing came out. Standing in complete silence they were both lost. He looked at her in disgust and left out of the bathroom. She didn't even chase after him, because what would she say? She slid down to the bottom of the shower and continued to cry. "Who hates me this much?"

Ivy paced the dimensions of their kitchen as if there were hidden clues in the cabinets. She made up some bizarre story to tell her job so she could skip work today because her eyes looked as if she was allergic to the tears that dripped down her face. Not having any recollection of when these pictures were taken, Ivy tried her hardest to think deeper into the situation. Forwarding the pictures to her email she saved the photos to examine them herself looking for small hints. It was extremely difficult because her ass and this guy's dick were plastered all over the place. Looking a tad bit closer, you could see something at the top left corner. Straining her eyes to get every angle, Ivy noticed it was her dressed balled up in the corner. Her adrenaline started pumping as she scrolled to the next picture. Able to point out the background she saw a Hennessy bottle in another corner. Paying close attention, she then realized that the hairstyle she had at that time was literally a couple of weeks ago. Thinking back to when she got it done. "BITCHHHHHH" Ivy hollered. She hasn't always been the brightest crayon in the box but she was putting two and two together and she came back with more than four.

Reviewing the pictures some more she became devastated. "How could I have been so naive and blind to all that was going down?" Calming herself down, Ivy couldn't fathom the whole ordeal. Nicole had always shown signs of being disloyal to get whatever it was that she wanted but she didn't ever think it would be her bit with Nic's venom. Now it was Ivy's turn to get poisoned by the crafty snake. A million "Why's" kept popping up in Ivy's tiny head. "Why is she trying to sabotage my relationship? Shit, why is my best friend trying to hurt me period?" So many thoughts ran through her mind and for the first time, when it came to Nicole, she didn't know how to react.

Chapter 18

Ivy sat wrecking her brain about how she even let Nicole catch her slipping like this. "How in the hell did she know Mik was at our place? The bitch probably knew he was in there beating my ass and didn't come and help. Shit she was probably fucking him too. Some friend. Jamila has to know something, anything. She and Nicole had done some scandalous shit to people and she'd be the first to know." Calling her cellphone with hopes she would know something, and not any made up bullshit, she answered on the first ring. "Vee, you must've knew I was thinking about you" Jamila sang through the phone. Shocked at her introduction, Ivy laughed to hide her distress. "Yes! Girlfriend we haven't talked in weeks, what's been going on? How are the kids?" Jamila talked mad shit about Reese not being able to keep her mouth closed but she couldn't hold water either. "Everyone is cool but umm girlfriend I have a few things I need to let you in on. Keep cool though cause I know how your mouth can get" Jamila said in the sweetest tone. That confirmed everything Ivy needed to know. Her best friend indeed was fucking her man and setting her up in the process. "Girl, if ya ass don't start talking I'm hanging up" Ivy said in a joking manner but nothing was funny. "Ok so I was out a couple of days ago and I overheard a couple chicks talking at the bar.

They were real bad loud as if they wanted me to hear them. I wasn't listening at first until I heard Mik's name and how he's fuckin loud mouth Reese" Ivy busted out laughing because Jamila couldn't possibly think she gave two shits about Mik especially after he had beat her ass the other day. "See you think everything is funny when I'm being serious" clearly irritated that Ivy found this humorous. "Naw my bad but that doesn't surprise me at all but continue." "Ard, so the other one jumps in like yeah yeah I was fuckin him too and blah blah blah and then she said all he ever talked about was killing Jace's brother Jay a while back" that's when Ivy's whole face turned red and her stomach knotted. Speechless. She couldn't believe what Jamila just blurted out her mouth as if that was some regular shit to say. Sensing her discomfort, Jamila stopped talking. Dead silence for what felt like a lifetime, Ivy Jumped back from her chaotic thoughts and apologized blaming it on her watching something on television. "My bad girlfriend, now finish what you were saying." "You sure girl cause what I say next may take you over the top?" Ivy chuckled once again, "If it's about some more hoes Mik had or has been fuckin I'll pass." Jamila held the phone real tight and took a deep breath and just blurted it all out, "Jace and Nicole has been seen out on several occasions." Ivy actually did want to laugh this time because this wasn't brand new news to her. She actually caught them herself. Playing dumb Ivy had to give her a bogus reaction to act as if this was her first time hearing this. "Bitch what?!" Ivy gave much attitude and Jamila felt so bad after the words left her mouth. Holding back another set of tears, Ivy ended the call because she felt herself getting emotional again.

Not able to clear her mind, Ivy sat in total disbelief about the recent chain of events. She couldn't believe that the two people she cared about the most would both stoop so low to try and hurt her for no particular reason. Well, Jace had a reason but why Nicole? That was her friend. She never did anything like this before. Shit, in the past Nicole always tried to protect Ivy from Mik's lowdown, conniving, and emotionless ass. It just didn't make sense but distraught Ivy would figure it out. Mrs. Price then creeps into Ivy's mind. Maybe she could tell me some shit about her foul adopted daughter.

Jace was quickly losing his mind. First the news about Mik killing his brother and now Nicole sends him more pictures of his cheating woman and this obnoxious asshole. "Like were they setting me up?" Jace thought. Driving with no destination, he ended up at the cemetery. Locating his brother's tombstone in seconds, he sat in front of his brothers resting place and poured his heart out. Talking and smoking with his brother for hours. He laughed, cried reminisced on all the good and bad times. The sun started to wrap up his shift so the moon could take over and Jace remained still. Finally snapping out of his memory lane coma, he said his goodbyes. When he checked his phone he had literally a hundred missed calls and texts from Nicole. He felt that was strange and unusual. She had already pulled the cards on Ivy so what else did she possibly want. Panic covered him as he started thinking the worst, something could've happened to Ivy or his mother but she wouldn't be calling about his mom. Anxious to hear the story behind the hundred texts she had sent he called her up. "Why weren't you answering my fuckin calls" Nicole spat as soon as she picked up the phone. Taking the phone away from his ear he sat and stared at it as if she lost her mind. "You questioning me like you my bitch, chill with all that shawty" he snapped "I'm sorry, I was calling because Ivy came here flipping out about you finding out about Mik." Instantly getting tired of her feeding him all this negative shit, he cut her off. "Look Nicole, I appreciate all that you done to look out but I'm done hearing about Ivy or anything she's doing" Trying to keep him on the line she invited him over for dinner. That really was the reason she blew up his phone. Not understanding why he agreed to go over her house, the weed and him being in his feelings led him to her.

Chapter 19

Mrs. Price hummed as she flipped the last piece of catfish over and listened closely to the channel 10 news. Her daily ritual was cut short when she heard a knock at the front door. Probably one of these kids coming to get a hot plate. The days of her being a foster mother were over. She gave it all up after her husband Curtis died of lung cancer. Things just weren't the same without him. Nicole got lucky out of the batch of brats Mrs. Price took in. She actually adopted Nicole and raised her. She knew Nicole like she knew herself. Opening the door without acknowledging who it was, Mrs. Price eyes lit up when she saw Ivy's face. Considering, they hadn't seen each other in almost a year, they embraced each other with a long warm hug. Ivy always loved the vibe she felt when she was in Mrs. Price's presence.

"Aww suga, what a pleasant surprise, were you in the neighborhood?" Mrs. Price said shutting the door. Excited to have some company over, she headed to the kitchen to fix them a plate. "Yes Ma'am, had to drop a few things off to my grandma's and decided to stop by and see how you were holding up" Ivy spoke as she took a seat at the dinner table. Mrs. Price beamed with joy. "So happy you stopped by, tell your grandmother I send my love" Both women had sat and chit chatted over dinner like old friends. Ivy had to butter Mrs. Price up before she slid in with the questions she had about this bitch, Nicole. They have been friends damn near their whole lives and Nicole concealed so many secrets from Ivy but one person she didn't hide anything from was Mrs. Price. "So has Nicki been around lately to see you? Ivy couldn't hold back any longer. "No baby she hasn't been by to see me for some time now and every time I call her she seems so busy. Ever since she had that abortion and that young man disappeared on her she hasn't been the same and I know when my baby isn't taking care of herself. I pray she's doing okay every night." Mrs. Price gave Ivy more than she expected. "Actually the last time she was here we were lying in my bed and she cried those pretty eyes out about that boy". "What was his name again I always seem to forget" Ivy interrupted briefly "Jay" Mrs. Price said calmly. "Yeah Jay, but when she left I noticed she had left behind her medication." She turned around and pointed towards the television stand. "I left them right there for her in hopes she'll creep in here one night and take them with her".

Blinking a thousand times, Ivy had to make sure she wasn't dreaming. Mrs. Price gave her more than she could chew. Feeling like she got all that she needed she was about to wrap up there night. "Wait Baby, I have to get something from upstairs give me one second" disappearing into the darkness,

Ivy waited until she heard her footsteps get further and she tiptoed over to the television stand and picked up the medicine bottles. "ZOLOFT! CLOZAPINE! What the hell?!" Ivy sat them back down when she heard the footsteps getting closer again. "Ok I'm back! Now Ivy you have a better chance at seeing Nicki before I do, so I want you to give her this address. I got a call recently from the adoption agency and they shared with me that they finally got a tombstone for Karen. Now isn't that lovely? She can now go and see her and finally be at peace and bury that hate." "No problem Mrs. Price, It was great seeing you, I'll be sure to stop pass more often and I'll get this information to Nicki" Ivy gave her a kiss and hurried to her car.

Once in the car, Ivy needed some weed because she couldn't believe that Mrs. Price gave up so much tape. Piecing together their conversation, she couldn't believe Nicole had an abortion and didn't tell her. Also that the bitch was bipolar and suffered from depression. No wonder the bitch was always so moody. Now delusional needs to be added to her diagnoses. "But wait, wait she said bul name was Jay. Earlier Jamila said Mik had killed Jace's brother, Jay. "Oh my god was this the same Jay? What in the soap opera was going on?" Ivy had heard enough in one day. Lighting her blunt, she took a long pull and looked at the paper she had in her lap. Reading it twice as if she missed a word or something, Ivy choked on the smoke. The address was to the cemetery her mother was buried at and her mother's name was written at the bottom of the paper. Karen Smith.

Chapter 20

The liquor and drugs were getting the best of Mik all of a sudden. He was always high and when he added the liquor it turned him into a fake ass Hulk, bringing him unneeded attention. He had it out bad for Ivy and Jace and would let anybody, who seemed interested, know. Ivy had betrayed him twice. First and foremost, for leaving him alone in jail and secondly for dealing with his enemy. Mik couldn't believe her stupid ass. Reese had enough of this drunken fool in her crib and needed a way to get rid of him. Mik kept Reese around because he needed to know what everyone was whispering about and he wanted everyone to know what he had going on. Of course she came through every time and today was no different. As Mik sat lounging on the sofa smoking a cigarette, he started rambling about poor Ivy and Jace again. Exhausted from hearing their names so much, Reese usually toned him out until she heard, "KILL THEM". He mumbled a lot of bullshit when he was high but never had she heard him say he wanted anyone dead. Beads of sweat sat on her forehead and upper lip. She was scared shitless because she didn't need anything falling back on her. Hearing he killed Jay was kind of a rumor in the hood. Nobody was sure if it was true or not, but now it was confirmed.

"Thank God I did decide to cook" Nicole thought as she closed the oven door. "Jay would've been mad if I told him to come over, and when he walked in there was no food cooking." Showering quickly, she smoothed her body with coconut oil and let her long jet black hair fall pass her breast. Searching through her panty drawer, she chose to keep it simple with some black lace boy shorts and a tank top. Taking the food out of the oven, she sat his plate to the side. Cuddled up on the couch waiting for him, she decided to call Jamila up. Nicole wanted to brag so bad about how she got her man back, and that he was on his way over now. She decided to just keep her thoughts to herself for now. Continuing to watch television and wait for her man, hours passed and the television began to watch her. Dozing off she awoke later on and searched around her apartment for any trace of Jay, there was none. Checking her phone for any missed calls she came up short. "He never showed the fuck up" screamed Nicole. Growing tired of the same bullshit, she became extremely upset and outraged that she allowed herself to be played once again. An irate Nicole then started to take her rage out on her living room. Kicking her glass table first, she then followed up by knocking a painting off of the wall. Nicole was pissed! Next she grabbed a bat that she kept behind her front door like Mrs. Price had taught her years back. Effortlessly swinging, she took the bat to her sofa until her arms became sore from the repeated strokes. Nicole was zoned out but unsatisfied. With eyes zooming in on her flat screen television, she took the bat and smashed the helpless 42 inch device into what seemed like a million pieces. Finally exhausted and breathing heavily, she felt as if, she couldn't take anymore. Nicole was at her breaking point and couldn't stop the sweat and tears from falling. At this moment she didn't have any more fight in her. No wait that's a lie, she was just getting started.

Jace sat outside of Nicole's building for a good hour before he decided he couldn't walk in there. He knew Nicole's type and didn't want to have anything to do with her. He felt like a dickhead for even entertaining her and the thought of him coming over. He then thought about Ivy, even though he hated the ground she walked on at this point, he could never intentionally hurt her like that. Jace definitely felt like she needed to pay for all the hurt and humiliation she caused him, but not like this. Jace thought "I do wanna hit her where it hurts, but how?"...

Jay was left to die alone. It was the dead of winter so it was only a selected few of people roaming the streets and they all claimed to have not seen anything, CLASSIC! Jace couldn't come to grips that his only brother, the only person he trusted in this fucked up world was gone. None of this made any sense because Jay was always so careful in everything that he did. Something isn't adding up and Jace could feel it.

"Can we meet? I need to see you" Reese tried her hardest to hide her fear. "Ugh yeah cool, meet me at our spot in a hour" hanging up Reese had to tiptoe around her own damn house so Mik ass wouldn't ask her where she was going or better yet ask could he come. Jamila sat waiting for slow ass Reese. They had seen each other twice after their first encounter and were digging each other so Jamila was kind of hype when she called asking to see her. "Surprise, Surprise" "thanks for showing up on time and not having me waiting." Jamila said sarcastically. Noticing the discomfort in Reece's eyes she quickly sat her down and asked what was going on. Holding nothing back, "Mik wants Ivy and Jace dead" she blurted it out not recognizing her voice was on a thousand and half of the restaurant heard her. "BITCH WHAT" Jamila shouted just as loud. "Mik is a pill head and wants attention he's just talking girl. What you need to do is focus on getting his bum ass outta ya spot." Jamila hinted with a bit of jealousy. She did one hell of a job hiding her true feelings though. She was just as nervous as Reese. Mik was beyond hurt and y'all know what hurt people do? They hurt people. "Man, let me call Ivy".

Two blunts later Ivy still sat in front of Mrs. Price's house. She couldn't figure out all the current events that had taken place. "First my own best friend sets me up to get gang raped by two guys and takes pictures to send them to my boyfriend. Secondly, they start fucking around with each other and I catch them on a damn date. Thirdly, my ex shows up at my place and kicks my ass while I'm apparently knocked up and don't know by who. Fourth, I find out this bitch is on crazy meds because she's out of her goddamn mind. Let's see did I forget anything? Oh yeah my ex-boyfriend killed my new boyfriend's brother, yeah that's important! Then lastly but surely not least, my mother and Nicole's mother share the same name, which is blowing my fucking socks off! That isn't no damn coincidence." Ivy sat and replayed everything over and over in her mind as she was interrupting by her cell. "Who the fuck is calling me right now?" Ivy shouted as she searched for her phone. It was Jamila. "I'm pretty sure this bitch has another fucking story to tell. I wouldn't be shocked if Nicole put her up to calling me to see how I was holding up after all this." Ivy answered "Yo" Ivy said dryly. "Where you at come meet me its urgent" said Jamila. "I'm around, wassup?" Mumbled an upset Ivy. "No, Ivy seriously can you meet me at the bar around the corner from my house in 20 minutes?" Jamila pleaded. Not buying her dramatic scene but needing a shot of anything she agreed. She hung up and headed that way. Weed and liquor were no good for the baby but how it's looking a baby wouldn't be in her near future.

Chapter 21

Walking into the bar, Jamila was nowhere in sight. Ordering a double shot of Henny, Ivy made herself comfortable. Downing the brown liquid, she felt a warm tingle that lit her petite body up. Ordering another, she didn't recognize anybody around her so she eased up and sipped this one slow. Checking her watch she became furious, Jamila had her sitting in this hood ass bar with only one way in and one way out. Ten minutes and she'll finish her shot, and then she was ghost. Clearly it wasn't that important that she had me waiting. Getting up after fifteen minutes, Ivy was fed up. She searched her wallet for a loose bill and when she looked up, Mik was staring her dead in her eyes. Usually when one drinks, it gives them ample amount of courage that they normally don't possess sober, but not tonight. Ivy was the complete opposite; she didn't want any trouble with Mik. Looking around to see if there was a faster way for her to make her exit in the tiny bar, Ivy panicked. Not knowing what to do next, she sat back down on the bar stool slowly. Glancing down at her phone, Jamila had texted a bullshit story explaining she'd be on her way soon. "Yeah fuckin right! This bitch probably told him I was going to be in here waiting" she wiped her sweaty hands on her jeans hoping it would knock the edge off. Now Mik was making his way to the back towards her.

"Please Lord, don't let this dumb nigga do anything stupid in here" silently praying as she watched his every move. "Hi beautiful, can I get you a drink?" Mik said not taking his eyes of her. Kindly rejecting his offer with a "No thank you, I'm fine" Ivy sat nervously. As if he didn't hear her, he waved down the bartender and ordered two more double shots. "Here you go, take a shot with me for old times" Mik said as he lifted his glass. Just following his lead so he could leave her the fuck alone, they tapped glasses but Ivy didn't drink. She just kept thinking "WHAT A FUCKIN DAY". Smiling and making his exit, Mik strolled out of the bar as if he was a Detroit pimp, looking for his hoes and money. Taking a deep breath, Ivy thanked the lord that he didn't try any shit. Gathering her things for the second time, Jamila walks into the bar as if she owns it all loud and extra. Screaming Ivy's name, Jamila was clearly drinking already. Not speaking a word, Ivy dropped a twenty on the counter and grabbed her coat. Jamila called her name repeatedly but got no response as Ivy walked right past her. Once she made it outside, she scanned the block to see if anything looked out of place. Feeling that Mik was somewhere lurking, she decided to call an uber to her grandmother's house. She rarely went there so she was hoping nobody popped up giving her anymore surprises for the night.

Standing at the bar completely unclear of what had just happened; Jamila sat and ordered a few drinks. She couldn't keep her mind off of all the things happening around her. Some shit was bound to go down, she could feel it. Reese and Ivy both had ditched her randomly and she couldn't understand why because they both failed to give any excuses. Nicole crossed her mind and she hated how distant she had become. The liquor started taking effect and "Missing you" by Brandy, Tamia, Gladys Knight and Chaka Khan came through the speakers. Instantly getting rather emotional, she sang along...

"How could it be, that sweet memories would be all, all that we have left" ....

"Oh so he wants to shit out on ya kids huh? Nicole said matter of factly. "Y'all he just a fucked up person. They haven't done anything to him but he's hurting them because I don't wanna be with his clown ass no more and he's taking it out on my babies" Jamila said frustrated. Ivy and Nicole looked at each other as if they had a brilliant plan. Nicole ran into Mrs. May's house and came back fifteen minutes later holding a plastic bag. Ivy giggled all the way to her car. Jamila sat clueless as she watched Nicole head to the passenger side. Calling for Jamila to bring her ass on, Ivy drove to the nearest Petsmart and hopped out. Coming back bearing gifts with a smile on her face. Jamila still sat unaware as to why her friends kept giggling. "What the fuck

are y'all laughing at? And where we going? Jamila demanded answers. "You'll see when we get there" Ivy said sternly. All three of the girls got quiet wondering what the others were thinking. Noticing where they were pulling up to Jamila yelled "why are we the fuck here? Why you drive over here Ivy? I don't have shit to say to bul!" Jamila continues to yell and shout. "Girl shut the fuck up and just follow our lead" Ivy shouted back clearly irritated with Jamila dippy ass. Opening the car doors, both girls headed to the trunk and retrieve their goodies. Telling Jamila to get out the damn car, all three girls headed to Shawn's front door. Jamila was crying and bitching the whole 10 ft. to his front door as if they were going to kill him and stash the body. Nicole opened her bag and set it directly in front of the door. Ivy followed suit and emptied her goodies into Nicole's bag. Out of nowhere Nicole pulled a note from her back pocket. Fed up with the mystery game she read the note "YOU WANNA SHIT ON MY KIDS? IMA SHIT ON YOU!!!"

Jamila busted out laughing not believing how sick her friends were. Inside the bag, Nicole had gone into the house and lined the toilet with a plaster bag and shitted inside. While Ivy dumped dead white mice into the shit. She thought about the mice because she use to watch the boys in school feed them to the snakes. Overly excited, Jamila set the note next to the shit. Knocking and kicking on the front door, all three girls ran to the *car unable to control their laughter. They didn't pull off until he opened the door. Seeing his face, Ivy pulled off so fast. Ten minutes later, Shawn was blowing up Jamila's cellphone. "Oh my god y'all think he knew it was us? Jamila shouted in between tears. They laughed so hard their stomach hurt.*

"What happened to those days? We always had each other's back" Jamila questioned herself as she reminisced. Just as she wiped her teary eyes to order another drink, she felt a tap on her shoulder. Turning around to see who it was she couldn't believe her eyes.

Mik was fed up with the way shit was going and needed quicker results. He gave up on fucking with Ivy physically but wanted to aim for her mentally. He wanted to hit her where it hurt; make her feel the real pain. Fooling around with thoughts in his head, Mik tried to devise a plan...

Remembering that day crystal clear. Mik and Jay sat in the car discussing business as usual. Jace pulled up and they both hopped out the car. Kicking there shit, the passenger side window randomly rolls down and a brown skin chick tells him his phones are ringing. Getting a better view of the girl, Mik never forgot her face. So the night he ran into her he knew exactly who she was. Wasting no time, Mik was in her face and she

loved it. He didn't know what type of broad she was but it came
out the bitch was very resourceful.

As if he had an epiphany, he jumped out of the bed and searched for his phone. He knew exactly who he was going to use as bait.

Nicole had, had enough of everything and everybody. Shit just hadn't been the same and she was over it. Refusing to take her meds, she felt that she didn't need to be drugged up all the time and that she was on top of the world without them. Her damage wasn't done though. "How could they do me this way? After all we've been through? I can't believe them." Nicole replayed those questions in her head several times a day.

Chapter 22

Rolling over from her liquor coma, Ivy laid there rewinding the shenanigans she had endured in the past few months and fast forwarding to last night's bullshit. "This can't be my life right now" she thought as she listened to her grandmother moving around the house. It was a bright Saturday morning and she was probably in the basement washing clothes. Wanting to pick her brain, Ivy cleaned herself up and headed in her direction. Creeping up behind Mrs. May, Ivy knew she was going to catch her off guard and that's exactly how she wanted it. "Mom mom, tell me more about my mom" Ivy said in a demanding tone. Mrs. May's entire face showed her discomfort. "I knew she knew more than she led on" Ivy thought. "Child, we've talked about her a million and one times what else you want to know?" Fidgeting with the clothes she became tense. "I need to know all the stuff you've never told me?" Ivy nudged on. Knowing this day would come, Mrs. May pulled Ivy upstairs and sat her down. Fooling around in a trunk in the dining room, she located what she was searching for. Ivy started to grow impatient waiting for what seemed like hours. "Mom Mom, I'm out because I don't have time for you to be avoiding my questions" Ivy shouted as she stood to leave. "Sit ya ass down" Mrs. May commanded. Finally sitting beside her granddaughter, she opened the tiny box and slowly passed Ivy numerous newspaper clippings that read...

"Two Men Rob Multiple Banks".... *"One man found Dead, woman shot"*.... *"Pregnant Woman delivers baby after gunshot"*....

Ivy sat uninterested in the titles of the newspaper articles. "I don't care about nobody being shot or robbed. "Goddamnit Ivy, Read" Mrs. May snapped and quickly rose to get some air.

"Police say two men are wanted for multiple crimes including bank robberies and breaking and entering. Both men are believed to be armed and dangerous"

"David Richardson has been charged with first degree murder and countless bank robberies on the east coast. David's best friend, Isaac had been having a love affair with his girlfriend Karen, of four years. David had his suspicions but they were confirmed on Wednesday night when David caught Isaac and girlfriend on a date. Shooting both out of rage, David turned himself in after he learned that he killed his best friend and his girlfriend who was unbeknownst to him pregnant at the time. David received life without parole.

"The fatal shooting happen shortly after 5pm. Officers found Isaac Rivers, 30 in the driver's seat of the vehicle with a gunshot wound to the neck... Rivers pronounced dead at the scene authorities said....

"Woman rushed to the hospital with gunshot wound to the chest, delivers baby.... Arrest has been made.

Ivy let the tears blind her. She looked up and her grandmother's eyes matched hers. Trying to envision everything that happened, Mrs. May came over and cupped Ivy's face. "I wish y'all got a chance to meet each other, you have his entire face" letting the tears flow she waited for her grandma to finalize the story. "Baby your mother loved two men at once but it didn't help that they were best friends. David and Isaac were inseparable and truly were more like brothers. Karen came along and had David head over heels. Madly in love, they conceived a child who caused their relationship to strain and they drifted apart. Isaac would come home upset that his friend was having issues, which caused them to have problems with their illegal business. Karen needed a shoulder to lean on but more came of it besides conversation. David found out about their affair and threaten to kill them both. Karen became paranoid and took their daughter to a foster home where she knew she would be safe. That evening David got confirmation that the only people he cared about were together and he kept his word. Twenty four hours later your beautiful face entered this world. And the rest is history baby".

Blown away by all that she had heard, Ivy let everything sink in and had to throw up. Running to the bathroom, she dived head first into the toilet. Mrs. May was right behind her, standing over her and consoling her only grandchild, wishing things had turned out differently. Helping Ivy back downstairs, Mrs. May had more she needed to tell. "Grandma, why are you just telling me all this?" Ivy said between tears. "I tried to protect you from anything negative sweetheart" Mrs. May said holding Ivy's hands. Ivy finally registered all the information that was dropped into her lap and almost had a heart attack. "Hold the fuck up, are you telling me Nicole is my sister? Now I realize why you've called us sisters for all these years. Dropping fuckin hints all my life, what the fuck grandma?" Ivy's whole face was red. "Now you're getting out of line talking to me like that Ivy, you must've lost your goddamn mind" Mrs. May screamed "I can't believe you kept this from me" Ivy started crying again. From all the tears she cried over the last few days you'd think she have a river named after her by now. "So you're the woman who called Mrs. Price from the adoption agency?" Lowering her head, Mrs.

May didn't utter a word. Grabbing her things, Ivy slammed the door as she hurried to get out of her grandmother's house.

Jamila continued to call Ivy nonstop. She was still shocked that she totally ignored and left her last night. "I'm calling to see if you're straight. You left your car outside the bar last night and just wanted to see if you needed a ride to get it. Let me know." Jamila hit send. She called Reese and didn't get an answer from her either. "These bitches man"...

Ivy got to her car and was scared to get in. Mik's crazy ass probably left a bomb under my hood or some wacked out shit. Checking it, she finally started the car and noticed a note on the window. "Meet me at my office" looking around to see if she noticed any of the faces in the crowd, she sped off. "Why the fuck would he put a note on my car when he could have texted me? The weird stupid shit people do is beyond me" All Ivy wanted was some weed and her bed to calm her nervousness. Between all the shit with Nicole, Jace and Mik, she was on some fuck it all type of shit! Ivy couldn't help but to feel like they were all fucking crazy and she didn't want any parts of their circus act.

Curiosity always wins and Ivy headed in a whole different direction. She didn't plan on going but something led her there. The sun had run away and now the clouds were up there looking dreary and tired. Parking and getting out, she walked up to the gates. She hesitated at first but she had some shit to get off her chest. She promised that she wouldn't shed a tear, just go all out about her feelings. No words would come out the first five minutes. Ivy just stood there staring into space trying to figure out what to say. "I HATE YOU" she finally released some words. "I thought I knew you. Everything you've ever told me was a lie. Now I'm struggling and living with these lies. You've broken happy hearts with your stupidity as well as your selfish ways. You didn't care about anybody but yourself. How is that even possible for a woman with children? I HATE YOU!" Holding back the tears, Ivy felt her whole body about to explode. She was so angry, she kicked the tombstone. Instead of heading to Jace's office, she went to pay her ruthless mother a visit. "You ruined not only me and Nicole's life but you destroyed our fathers too. All this time you had me believing my father was killed in a car crash and you got Nicole's father sitting in fuckin jail for life behind your bullshit. We're both emotionally unattached behind your fucked up ways. Me and my sister have real life issues because of you. My own grandmother hid this shit from me to protect the perfect image I had of you, when you were the one who got her son killed. I hope that disease is still eating at your soul you sick bitch" Ivy kicked the tombstone once more and ran off to her car. She held her composure for as long as she could. Breaking down in the car, she tried to pull herself together.

Jace felt like he was losing everything including his goddamn mind. He had just hung up with his mother and she wasn't doing too well. Closing his eyes, he felt a calm come over him. Since he's been staying at his office, he hasn't had time to deal with anybody and their lies, so he thought. He could hear a slight murmur at the door followed by a knock. Uninterested by whomever was at the door; he ignored them and kept quiet. Cursing under his breath that his secretary didn't turn them away. The knock continued and got louder. Noticing that they weren't leaving any time soon, he yelled for whomever it was to come in. Walking in with a half-smile, Reese could see the stress written all over his face. She was kind of disappointed that he wasn't so enthused to see her. Reese and Jace had known each other for a few years now. They casually met through a mutual friend at a party. Conversation and drinks were flowing and one thing led to another, eight hours later Jace was leaving money on her night stand. Being as though Jace was from across the bridge, Reese thought she caught a big fish and thought she could hide her whorish ways. WRONG! She had him fooled but his brother quickly let him know the bitch was bad for business. Little conversations here and there, and a few late night specials but nothing had or were going to become of them. Reese was okay with that, but Jace not giving her a friendly smile or a gesture led her to believe that anything they had going on sexually had been buried along with her hopes of something more. "No love huh?" Reese said still smiling. Jace was pissed she had the audacity to show up at his place of business. Her vibe wasn't off but something was up, he could feel it. "Naw babygirl, everything straight! Wassup witchu tho? To what do I owe the pleasure?" Giving her his fakest smile. She started talking but he heard nothing of what she was saying. "Just was in the neighborhood, thought of you and decided to come and say hello! I hope that's not a problem?" Reese said. "No, no you good!" But my question to you is "WHAT ARE YOU REALLY HERE FOR?"

Reese felt a tad bit anxious after she realized that this wouldn't be an easy task like she had originally thought it would be. Jace was far from a square like he had led on. He knew something was up. "I'm really here because I really wanted to see you. I miss you!" She said with a devilish grin. Jace knew that was bullshit but he let it slide for the moment but for the time being, he was gonna let her show him how much she missed him. "Come show me than". Reese didn't have sucking his dick on her agenda but she didn't mind because it was always a pleasure in the end.

Chapter 23

"Hey, Good Afternoon, this is León Matsinger calling from Johnson and Johnson. I'm Nicole's boss over here at the company and we've been very concerned about Nicole. She has neglected all her duties and no one seems to be able to reach her. Last time we spoke she advised us that her grandmother had passed away and she needed a few days off. That was over a month ago and we wanted to know if she needed our help in anyway. Please give me a call at your earliest convenience at 555-555-5555. Thank you and have a great evening.

Ivy deleted the message as soon as she heard Nicole's name and continued on with her day. Jace was on her visiting list for the day. They haven't had any contact with one another since that morning he confronted her about Mik. At this point she wanted her man and her life back, but if he wanted it to be over so that he could be with this bitch Nicole then he would have to tell her to her face.

"What am I gonna do about this goddamn baby? At this stage bringing a child into this world will only complicate things. Jace and I aren't at our best and I doubt we'll ever be. So what the fuck do I do?" Ivy noticed Jace sitting in his truck as she pulled up to his office. A grey impala pulled off as soon as she parked as if on cue. "That better not been no bitch" Walking to his window he signaled for her to get in. She hoped he was in a better mood today, so that they could figure some things out. Ivy was going to try her hardest to push past the clown shit that's been going on and talk like two adults. It was just up to him to act the same. As soon as her butt hit the seat he asked her what she wanted. Surprised at his response she calmed herself and thought of the right choice of words to say to this piece of shit.

"You're asking me why I'm here as if I killed your puppy or something. When you don't fully know the answers to things that's when you start asking questions, right?! Furthermore, you let a nutcase come and destroy the good shit that we were building!" Jace sat with a blank stare on his face as if he'd rather watch paint dry, rather than, listen to her fake ass lecture. "We both let her manipulate us. Believing shit that wasn't true and doing shit that we normally don't do. How you let a stranger fuck us up Jace? HOW? I trusted her so much that I allowed her to feel comfortable enough to drug me and have me raped on the account of her sick twisted mind". Her eyes filled with tears. Jace started shifting in his seat. "You knew this whole time and didn't utter a fuckin word to me about it because you just thought I was out here fuckin niggas because that's what she told and showed you" Jace sat blowing up inside. He wanted to hug her so bad because at that moment he knew she was speaking the truth but he wouldn't dare let his guard down. "Ask me am I ok!" Ivy said waiting for him to say something but he came back with nothing. He sat staring out the window as if none of what she said fazed him. Ivy gripped the door handle before opening it. "By the way, I'm pregnant! Go ask Nicole who the father is" slamming the door as hard as she could she ran to her car and sped off. Jace sat dumbfounded. He didn't know what to do or say at this moment. Ivy was his girl and this Nicole bitch came out of nowhere but what was her motive behind everything?

"Yo shawty, where you at? I wanna see you"...

CHAPTER 24

Nicole was over everything with Jay. This motherfucker wanted to play cat and mouse games but she was done being the cat. Her cell phone started buzzing again. Mrs. Price had been blowing her up for the past two days. Right now wasn't the time to communicate with anybody that would have her losing focus. Grabbing her phone to silent the ringer she noticed it wasn't Mrs. Price but a number that she didn't recognize. Quickly answering before the caller decided to hang up, she was curious to know if it was Jay finally calling. "Hello!" She said in a sexy tone trying to disguise her excitement. "Aye Nic, where you at? I gotta holla at you about something" noticing the voice her tone changed. Agreeing to meet the caller soon, she hopped up and ran to her bedroom to get dressed. Pulling up in front of the location, Nicole got a gut feeling that something wasn't right. As soon as the thought crossed her mind she went to put the car in drive but the passenger door swung open. Scared shitless she jumped. "Chill I ain't gone hurt you Nic" Mik laughed as he shut the door. "Pussy, what the fuck is wrong with you? Don't just be hopping in my shit like that!" Slightly annoyed Nicole pulled off totally turned off and would rather not hear what he had to say. "Ard, this is what we gonna do" Mik said proudly. "We? Nigga who? You said you had to holla at me about something. Not we gotta do something. I can't believe I even met ya clown ass" Nicole was irritated and it showed. "Bitch what? Nic I will smack the shit outta ya sneaky ass. I see through all that fake shit. Don't front for me. "WE" the same type of person. You want that nigga Jace bad and Ivy is the only thing standing in your way, you'll do just about anything to get her outta here" Mik said without taking a breath. Sitting real quiet Nicole rolled her eyes. "Like I said this is what WE gonna do!" As if he was huddled in a circle with his high school basketball team Mik drew up a plan.

Reese regretted ever talking to Mik that night at the club. He was loud, cocky and flat out disrespectful as fuck. Realizing that he only was using her she tried her best to get him to leave her the fuck alone. She had called Mik over five times and got the voicemail every time. Kind of pleased that she didn't have to deal with him at this moment, but she knew he would be on her line very soon.

Mrs. May was so overwhelmed with guilt; she didn't even try to reach out to her granddaughter knowing that she needed space and time. Mrs. May never wanted to keep the truth from Ivy and decided that there was one other person who deserved to know the truth as well. Nicole sat and released smoke into the air as she watched the youngbul she brought home with her last night get dressed. Seeing Mrs. May's name across her screen was strange but she answered with hopes that it was news about Ivy magically disappearing. "Hey Nicole! It's Mrs. May, how are you?" "Hey grandma, I'm fine! Are you okay? Something wrong?" Pretending to be concerned, Nicole listened closely not missing a word. "I'm good baby; I need to speak with you and Ivy in person soon!" "Oh this old bitch must not know I'm ready for her granddaughter to be gone. A meeting? I think the fuck NOT! But on second thought, this may be the perfect solution to fix all my problems" Nicole thought as she told Mrs. May she'd stop pass tomorrow. Nicole had been on a rampage to get revenge on Ivy. Maybe seeing her face to face wouldn't hurt.

"Pull back around real quick" Jace spoke into the phone. Moments later, Reese creeps back up the block searching for Ivy's car. She didn't have any beef with Ivy but if she had seen her even two feet near her man, World War III definitely would've popped off. This time he got out of his truck and hopped in Reese's car. "Okay baby girl, I need you more than ever right now" Jace said with the most sincere facial expression. Shaking her head yes, Reese decided at that moment that whatever Jace said goes. "I know that nigga Mik sent you here" Jace started talking noticing the surprised expression that crossed Reese's face and she couldn't hide it. "It's cool I understand, this how shit goes. But right now I need you to pick a side". Reese already was all ears. "I don't even like Mik, I can't." "Shhh baby girl, I said I understand" Jace put his index finger to her mouth. "I want you to keep your fuckin mouth shut, unless you're telling me the whereabouts of this faggot" Reese just wanted to find a rock and hide. She kept asking herself "how in the hell did I get my loud mouth into this shit."

Finally breaking the ice, Ivy broke down and called her grandmother. In the midst of all the dumb shit that transpired, she failed to share her news with Mrs. May. Exposing everything to her grandmother may be a relief for her, considering the last several months had been hell. Mrs. May was happy that Ivy had called. She didn't mention that she had spoken to Nicole because she didn't want Ivy flying off the coop again. Ivy needed to speak to her grandmother but decided to save all of the good stuff for when she saw Mrs. May in person; Ivy was thrown off when she got a text messages from an unknown number.

"Hey, this is Jade. Jamila was rushed to the emergency room. The doctors aren't telling me anything"

Making a u turn in the opposite direction, Ivy ceased everything she was doing and rushed to be by her friends' side. Brushing past several people, Ivy hurried to the front desk demanding answers. Once upstairs, roaming the halls for Jamila's room she spotted Jade.

"What's going on? What are they saying it is?" Jade just shook her head No! Ivy was confused so she went and searched for her own answers. Slowly walking into the room what she saw was a major surprise. Jamila was beaten badly. Her sandy brown hair was ruffled up and her nose looked as if it could have been broken. Both of her eyes were black, blue and swollen shut. Her cheeks looked as if she had stashed some peanuts on both sides like the chipmunks did. Gasping for air, Ivy covered her mouth. She had flashbacks of when she visited Nicole in this same hospital and couldn't stomach seeing her friends like this. Jamila was beaten badly, way more severely than Nicole had been in the past. Opening her eyes slightly, tears formed and trickled down her bruised face when she recognized her friend standing in front of her. She looked as if she'd rather be dead. Looking away from Ivy, she felt ugly and embarrassed. Immediately feeling her friend's pain, she walked over and palmed her hand. "Jamila I am so sorry that this happened to you. I'm sorry that I've been acting like a bitch". Holding her tears in, she felt Jamila tighten her grip and they cried together. Finally after twenty minutes of silence, Jamila gained enough energy to speak. "Nicole, Nicole and Mik" she stuttered as she tried reaching for her ice water. Helping her out, Ivy placed the straw to her mouth. "Nicole and Mik did this to me Vee" turning the television off to hear her clear. "They did what to you Jamila?" Ivy leaned in closer to Jamila. "Nicole and Mik did this to me" struggling to speak "they wanted me to set you up and I told them to kiss my ass and then they beat my ass" Jamila chuckled a little through the pain. Trying to finish her sentence, Ivy stopped her. "Thank you, I swear I owe you" sitting back, Ivy held her friend's hand tighter for the rest of the night. "Oh so they're sending messages huh?" Ivy's mind went into overtime and she wasn't sure what time her shift would be over.

Mrs. May was ecstatic that Nicole had kept her promise and stopped past. She was ready to explain to her all the things that she kept bottled up all of these years. "I'm so happy you decided to come baby" Mrs. May smiled passing Nic a glass of wine. "Yeah I didn't have any plans, plus you seemed so eager to get me over here, so here I am" she sarcastically spoke as she grabbed the glass. Sensing her bad vibe, Mrs. May ignored it and continued to roam the home. Ivy was on turtle time and Nicole was ready to go. Noticing her becoming uneasy in her seat she decided that maybe it was best that Ivy wasn't present. "Umm okay so Nicole, I have a few things I need to fill you in on. I need you to be completely calm and to hear me out" Nicole sat calmly and quietly staring at Mrs. May as if she had ten heads. "Come on grandma; please don't beat around the bush! Say what you gotta say so I can get outta here" clearly agitated. "I know you had a rough hand dealt to you as a child but I promise your mother never intended for it to happen that way" Mrs. May spoke in a low tone. "No disrespect to you but fuck my mother! If that's what you called me over here for than save it" Nicole grabbed her things to leave. "Baby, Karen is your mother too! You and Ivy are sisters!"

Nicole stopped in her tracks and turned and looked at Mrs. May as if she had seen a ghost. She had heard stories about how Karen was this and how Karen was that as if she was some fucking saint. That bitch wasn't anything but a whore. Immediately, Nicole felt overwhelmed and all of these emotions started to hit her at once. She hated Mrs. May for bringing it up now. Speaking in a harsh tone, Nicole lashed out. "She left me to rot in hell while this stuck up bitch got pampered with the best of everything. While I was tryna keep men off of me she slept well at night. While they were shacked up eating steaks and shit I was praying I got a piece of bread for dinner. How that happen? Tell me was I not good enough? I was her first child; she could've come back for me! She turned her back on me when I needed her the most". Mrs. May tried to console a hurt Nicole but she wouldn't let her. Nicole started trembling "DONT FUCKIN TOUCH ME" she screamed. "My life was shit literally. You knew this and never came to save me. Precious Ivy is gonna pay for my mother's fucked up ways since she can't. She's the reason my mother left me anyway" screaming at the top of her lungs "Ivy where are you?" She continued to chant. Mrs. May was nervous because she wasn't sure what Nicole's next move would be. She watched as Nicole turned into a completely different person before her eyes. "Ivy's been causing me problems since I met her ass. First my mother, then my man. The bitch has got to go". Nicole then kicked the television and picked up anything that was in her sight and threw it. Mrs. May ran into the kitchen to call for help as she cried for Nicole's pain. Regretting that she tried to bring the sisters together realizing that they were better off apart.

Mik was strolling around as if he owned the fucking world. Head held high, high off life. He was one step closer with his plan to shit on Ivy and Jace's perfect fairytale. They both felt like they were untouchable and he had to prove them wrong. Reese and Nicole were holding him down and that's all he cared about...

Overhearing Jace slander his name sent a chill through Mik's spine. He knew that he didn't have any love for him but for him to disrespect him took shit to another level. Mik knew that he would have to watch out for this nigga. Ain't no telling what he got up his sleeve.

Jace kept thinking of all the shit Ivy had said before she hopped out of his truck. He couldn't believe she was pregnant and how the fuck was he supposed believe her. Putting his pride in the back seat, he sent her a text telling her to meet him at home.

Ivy hadn't left Jamila's side. She felt responsible for the fucked up things Mik and Nicole had done to her. Reflecting on all the chaos, she realized that everyone that held value in her life were basically causing the most damage. For the life of her she couldn't understand why. A text from Jace and Reese walking into the room interrupted her train of thought. Jamila was awoke and doing better but the look on Reese's face shook the whole room. "Reese you looked spooked sis, you got something you wanna say?" Ivy stood over her waiting for her response. Reese broke down. Ivy looked at Jamila for answers but she too was lost at the sudden outburst. "Ivy, I'm so sorry I swear I didn't wanna have anything to do with it. Mik put me up to setting Jace up" she cried. "BITCH HE DID WHAT?" Ivy yelled. The nurses rushed into the room after hearing all the commotion. "Excuse me; we need you guys to keep it down in here. If not you'll be asked to leave". Waiting for the nurses to flee the scene, every nerve in Ivy's body stung. She knew Mik was fucked up but what in the psycho. "Reese on my dead father's grave I will kill you myself if ya busted ass don't start explaining yourself". Jamila tried calming them down but she wasn't physically capable. "Ok so I was letting Mik stay at my place when he came home. All he talked about was you and how you shitted on him and how you weren't getting away with that shit. So one night he comes in whispering all types of bullshit. Somehow he seen you and Jace together at home and he flipped out" said an emotional Reese. "But how the fuck does he know where we live?" Now she understood why he came and beat her ass that night. "Him and Jace's brother Jay use to be friends before Jay got killed. Word on the street is that Mik is the one who killed him"...

Seated in the visiting room, Ivy continued to drill Mik on why they were charging him for murder. He kept dancing around the question saying that they didn't have any witnesses or evidence.

Closing her eyes to let all this register. Ivy couldn't catch a break. When it rains it damn sure pours. "That was you at Jace's office wasn't it?" Ivy opened her eyes and dug holes in Reese as she walked closer. Her adrenaline rose and her heart started pounding. Reese never backing down from a fight had to bow out this time because she wouldn't win. She knew she fucked up and deserved whatever ass whooping that had her name on it. "The plan was for me to fuck him like old times and get as much info out of him as I could but when I got there I couldn't go through with it" Reese confessed. "Jace and I was a thing before y'all ever met and Mik used that to his advantage". Ivy had heard enough, she kissed Jamila goodbye and shot Reese a real nasty look and walked out the hospital room. She drove home in silence as she thought about what would happen on the next episode of her soap opera life.

Nicole planted herself in the middle of Mrs. May living room floor. She sung a soft lullaby that Mrs. Price sang to her as a teenager. Tears flowed down her eyes as she released every word. Watching from a distance, Mrs. May let her be alone. Calling Ivy and Mrs. Price numerous times, she gave up after not being able to get anyone on the phone. Then she heard whispers. "Jay please come home! I need you, and so does the baby! Ivy will never love you as much as I do! Can you please listen to me? Trust me! Jay! Jay! Don't leave me alone, stay please!" Nicole cried and rocked back and forth. She had lost her mind.

Nicole has been calling Jay nonstop all day and he didn't answer not one call. Furious, she needed to hear his voice or, even better, see his face. She left Mrs. May's house completely vexed that she had to hear that bogus story. Heading straight to where she thought Jace was, Nicole had a task that she needed to complete. Knocking on the door she waited for him to answer.

Ivy's car was nowhere in sight, so that confirmed that she wasn't going be a problem. It took him a century to open up. As soon as he laid eyes on Nicole, his whole mood switched up. Pushing past him, he attempted to grab her. You could tell in his eyes that he had been drinking and smoking. Constantly moving around, he gave up on trying to get a hold of Nicole. "Won't get rid of me that fast again" she silently thought as she dropped her bag near the sofa.

"Why are you here? I've told you this ain't that shawty" Jace said with a slurred tone. Ultimately hurt, Nicole attempted to kiss him. He pushed her away as if she had some incurable disease. Feeling abandoned, Nicole instantly started swinging, hitting and kicking. She wouldn't stop. Gripping her wrist trying to control her, Jace noticed something very different but familiar about her. For a quick second she could pass for Ivy. Thrown off by the resemblance, he let her wrist go and sat down. Nicole never the one to let an opportunity pass, she walked up and straddled Jace. She then planted a kiss on his soft full lips. Nicole was mesmerized by how quickly his attitude had changed. "Jay, I've missed you so much baby! Why would you ever leave me like that?" She whispered in his ear.

CHAPTER 25

Jace set puzzled by the kiss, but also by her calling him by his brother's name. Pushing her off of him, you could see the discomfort in his body. "Chill with calling me my brother's name, you getting outta pocket" "Jay! Seriously I am not in the mood for your childish ass games right now" Nicole shouted so every word she spoke was clear. "Bitch are you delusional or are you hard at hearing? I ain't fuckin Jay" Jace shouted a little louder this time. Nicole's anger was growing as fast as a wildfire. "So you just gonna try and keep this secret identity shit up because you don't want ya precious Ivy to feel a way about you fuckin the both of us? Then you acting as if you don't know me" Nicole's eyes start twitching and she still couldn't comprehend what he was saying to her. Pacing back and forth she started talking to herself. "Look shawty I don't know what the fuck ya problem is, but I ain't Jay and I have never fucked you." He spoke but none of his words were registering. "Jay is my brother but he was murdered a few months back in a playground down South Philly. It was plastered all over the news for like a month. I don't know how or why you got us mixed up or who told you what, but I aint him" Jace spoke clearly sobering up. "On some real shit, if you didn't want to be with me anymore after I had the abortion, that's all you had to

126

say. But just up and leaving was some real clown shit Jay. Then you start fuckin my best friend, real fuckin foul" Jace was becoming real impatient with Nicole and this fucked up fairytale ending she kept talking about. He sent Ivy another text to see where the hell she was at so that she could tame her friend. "Look, I ain't got nothing for you, you can let yourself out" he said as he lay back on the couch. The steam could be seen coming out of Nicole's ears, nose and mouth. She stood in the middle of the living room fuming. Quickly picking up her bag, she walked back over to the sofa. By this time Jace was laid out with his eyes closing as a result of the alcohol and weed taking over. In one swift motion, she pulled a dull object out of her bag and stood over him. Feeling her presence over him he opened his eyes a second too late. She drove the sharp knife into his broad body.

Ivy didn't know what to expect when she walked into their home. She automatically prepared for a yelling and screaming match because that was all they had been doing nowadays. As Ivy walked into their home she immediately saw Jace stretched out on the couch with the music blasting, and a bottle of Henny resting on the floor. Every light was on throughout the condo and you could smell the weed aroma in the air. Calling his name loudly over the music, Ivy became frustrated because he was clearly ignoring her. Walking closer to him she noticed his eyes wide open. "So you don't hear me fuckin calling you" but as the words left her mouth, she saw blood on his t-shirt and a small puddle dripping from the couch to the floor. Her heart skipped a beat and she couldn't even scream his name. Whispering so only those two could hear "Jace, Jace! Can you hear me? Get up please! Ivy grabbed his cell phone and called 911. Trying to stay calm and wait for help she noticed a ripped up picture lying next to the bottle of alcohol.

Mrs. May had gone upstairs to rest herself after the long night she had with Nicole. No one ever called her back so she left Nicole alone and went on to bed, praying that these two girls found forgiveness within one other as well as their mother. In a deep sleep, she awoke to her bedroom door being opened. She knew it was Nicole so she didn't bother to turn on the light. Their shadows were the only things seen in the pitch black room with a hint of light from the streetlights outside the windows. "Come on Baby, you can sleep with me" not saying a word Nicole slid right beside Mrs. May. Only moments later all you could hear in the dark room was muffled screams. Nicole had placed the pillow over Mrs. May's face. She kicked and swung but her old body didn't stand a chance again Nicole's athletic build. After a good three minutes, Mrs. May gave up the fight. Standing to leave, she smiled with tears in her eyes. She left just as quietly as she came.

Reese planned to stay with Jamila for the night. The doctor didn't want to discharge her because she still had massive swelling. Chit chatting about small things, their conversation was interrupted by Reese's phone. She stepped into the hallway making sure her voice was at a low tone. It was Mik finally returning her call. Wanting to ignore him she thought twice because that would've drawn suspicion on her part. "Where the fuck is you at" he spat as soon as he heard her voice. "I had to stop past my sisters, I'm on my way in now" she said nervously. "Hurry the fuck up" he shouted and then hung up. Growing restless with his bullshit, she prayed this would be the last time she talked to him.

Mik didn't trust Reese. Something was off about her energy and he needed to see her face to face to make sure he wasn't tripping. He trusted that Nicole was able to handle anything he threw her way because the bitch was just like him, ruthless and heartless. Letting himself into Reese's house he decided to take a shower. Getting restless and impatient he searched for his phone to call her again. "An hour had gone by and the sneaky bitch should've been home" he thought as he saw that Nicole had texted him. He smiled from ear to ear as his dick got hard. The plan had worked and now he was satisfied. Forgetting all about Reese he laid back with joy. As if on cue, all Mik heard was a loud boom and the front door came crashing in. Cops rushed through the house like some roaches when you turn the kitchen light on. Totally caught off guard, Mik just dropped to the floor. He smiled because every goal he set, he accomplished. He didn't care if he fucked up lives because his was already fucked up. You get what you deserve! Reese stood outside waiting for them to escort Mik into a police car. They both locked eyes and grinned at one another. Prior to her seeing Ivy at the hospital, she had held a very informative conversation with a guy she had recently been sleeping with and as fate would have it, he turned out to be a cop. She started asking for direction and he put her on the right path. Reese had explained everything to Jamila. She told her everything that Mik had disclosed about him killing Jay and how Jace and Ivy were next. What Mik didn't know is that Reece had recorded the whole temper tantrum he had at her house that day. She explained that the plan originally wasn't to set him up but after she saw what he and Nicole had done to Jamila, she knew she didn't have a choice.

The ambulance had arrived fast and started to work on Jace. Keeping him alive long enough until they reached the hospital. They wouldn't allow Ivy to ride inside with him so she followed closely in her car. The doctors went straight into an emergency surgery. He had been stabbed in his lungs twice. Four times in his ribs and three times in his neck. Alerting his mother on what was happening, Ivy was rather calm. Noticing that her grandmother had called her a billion times, not wanting to wake her at this hour she decided to call in the morning. Quietly seated in the waiting area she had flashbacks of walking in on him. Going into her pocket she had remembered the shredded picture. It was the picture of her and Nicole in Cancun. Her blood started to boil and the hate she had for this bitch was higher than the dope head seated across from her. Trying to keep her composure in the hospital, Ivy knew this bitch was delusional and fucked up in the head. Hours later, the short chubby Jewish doctor wobbled his way over to Ivy. His face showed no sympathy or remorse. Expecting the worst, Ivy just lowered her head ready to take on the harsh news. "Ms. Smith, your boyfriend is doing better!" Ivy instantly started crying. Thank god she came home when she did. "Ma'am he's in the ICU right now. We want to keep a close watch on him." He spoke proudly. "Go on home and come back in the morning to see him" thanking the doctor continuously, Ivy called Jace's mother to let her know how everything went. Her flight wasn't due until tomorrow afternoon. Wanting to be by his side when he woke up, an upset Ivy didn't want to leave but she obeyed the doctor's wishes and headed home.

It had been a little after one in the morning and a random number was calling her phone. It's was Reese screaming happily, "they got his ass." Instantly ready to curse this bitch out for dialing her number after a certain hour, an irritated wondered what was going on. "Why the hell is she saying they got his ass? I know that bitch was lying to my face to protect her own ass. Ima kill this bitch" thought Ivy. "Do you hear me Ivy?" Reece kept yelling into the phone "they just locked Mik's dumbass up". Confused at this point, Ivy didn't know what drug Reese was high off. "Mik, Ivy! They just booked him at my house" Ivy's stomach knotted. Her thoughts ran wild. A joy came over her body as she imaged them catching his devilish ass but she was sad that she wasn't the one behind him being put in jail. Forgetting her recent scenarios about what she was going to do to Reese, she headed to her car. Nicole had been seated outside of the hospital watching and waiting to see if she saw Ivy. The knife sat right beside her in the passenger seat. Her eyes were cherry red and her hair was wild and untamed, sort of resembling the wild animal she had been acting like. Peeping Ivy finally, she noticed that she was untroubled. That sent a disappointing wave through her body. She wanted to show her face but this wasn't the right time.

Opening the front door, Ivy had tripped over something but she couldn't tell what it was. Furthering her steps she continued to trip over a lot of shit. Her grandmother was a rather neat freak so she didn't understand what the fuck was up with all the junk thrown around. She had driven to her grandmother's straight from the hospital because she didn't want to be alone. Keeping quiet, Ivy creep upstairs to Mrs. May's bedroom. She usually slept in her old room but tonight she didn't want to be alone. Normally she wouldn't wake her up but she needed someone to talk to. "Mom Mom, get up! Grandma wake up!' Ivy continued to shake Mrs. May but she didn't budge. At that moment Ivy knew something wasn't right. Getting into bed, she cuddled up next to her grandmother. Grabbing her hand she still felt warm. Ivy laid there feeling nothing; every emotion in her body was gone. At this point she had given up.

CHAPTER 26

It had been a tough six months. With the New Year finally around the corner, Ivy was excited because she and Jace has surpassed all of the bullshit and decided to start over. The beginning of the road was rocky after Ivy delivered their daughter Jacie, prematurely, but Ivy couldn't be happier. Jace had been discharged from the hospital literally five days before Jacie was born and by the grace of God he was there to watch the birth of his baby girl. Jace couldn't help but to fall in love with Ivy all over again after witnessing the delivery. Ivy was still in a depressed state about her grandmother, some days were better than others, but Jace promised himself he would help her through it. On several occasions they both wanted to give up because they had lost so much but, they gained control back over their lives and vowed to iron out all the wrinkles. Time has a way of healing old wounds, but those wounds always turn into scars and every time you glance at those scars you're reminded of the battles that led you to the victory. They put aside all of the things that happened and decided to start over; agreeing to move on with life and to keep the past in the past. Jace was not as forgiving as Ivy though. He still had dreams and nightmares of all of the things that led up to this point. He was grateful to still be here but he couldn't help but to hurt for the people who couldn't be. "I won't be out too long, you sure you'll be able to handle her without me?" Jace questioned. "I only dropped her once, I'll try not to do it again" they both laughed. Jace kissed both of his girls and left the house.

It's was 1:20am and the club was packed. Nicole stumbled her drunken ass to the bar. "Henny & Coke" she yelled to the bartender. The liquor had taken over her body hours ago and she needed to take control over one of these guys. The weed she smoked earlier mixed with the alcohol had her horny and she needed to have some fun. Sipping on her drink she noticed a tall guy dressed in all black at the end of the bar. "BINGO" downing the rest of her drink she walked over to him to get a better look. His back was to her and she leaned in and whispered in his ear "hey you" he quickly turned around and you would've thought Nicole seen a ghost. "Uh Uh Jace, hey I didn't know that was you. I'm sorry! She stuttered. "Aww shit, wassup Nic. How you been? I've been looking all over for you!" Jace smiled so bright. "Me?" She said shocked. "Yeah you, let's get some more drinks" he flagged down the bartender. Nicole sobered up quick and wondered why the fuck he was looking for her. "So I wanted to personally thank you for everything. I suspected Vee was cheating on me. But listen to this, the baby isn't even mine" Jace hung his head low. "Look Nic let's get outta here and go somewhere and talk."

"Oh now this nigga wanna talk? Its 2am, the only thing we talking about is what hotel we going to!" She thought to herself as she followed him out of the club. "So where we going?" "It's a surprise" Jace said with a seductive look on his face as he led her to his car. Nicole's mind was racing a mile a minute; she couldn't believe this was happening. "I knew he would come to his senses" she thought as she smiled from ear to ear. "What u smiling for?" He questioned. "Oh nothing it's just a beautiful night. She said trying to wipe her happiness off her face.

"Aight, I'll be right back let me talk to my man right quick" as he closed the door. Nicole thought, as she sat back. "Is this real?" She couldn't believe what was happening. She closed her eyes and could envision, literally, the taste of his dick as she fantasized about it. Jace got right back in the car smiling. "Oh I gotta show you something real quick" he said as he pulled out his phone. Nicole sat there high off life. This moment meant everything to her. She finally had her man back! Passing Nicole the phone, Jace had a video up for her to watch. She pressed play and her stomach dropped. It was her on camera stabbing him after he told her to get out of his house. Next she saw herself leaving out of Mrs. May's house with the pillow she had smothered her with throwing it in the trash in the front of her house. Speechless, Jace decided to talk for her. "So Ivy told me to let everything go and let your crazy ass suffer in peace alone.

I thought about it a few times but I couldn't just react off of one person's opinion, so I reached out to a few other people. I thought about Mik, but god rest his soul he didn't make it two months upstate. Then I came across someone else that was sort of close to you." "Jace, I promise that I am" Nicole eyes started tearing up. "Please don't interrupt me again Nicole!" Jace said calmly before he started talking again. Nicole didn't close her eyes. If she was going out it was going to be with her showing she wasn't afraid of him or anybody else. Just then she glanced to the left of her and noticed a picture on Jace's dashboard. Squinting her eyes to see, completely ignoring Jace's speech, she laid eyes on the man she had been searching for. Tracing back to the conversation her and Jace had in his house about Jay being dead. During their conversation she had thought it was bullshit, until she laid eyes on his obituary. She looked at his smile, as she rested her eyes on the dates. Tears formed in her eyes and she started crying uncontrollably. May 8th was the day she had gotten her abortion. Thrown off by her sudden emotions, Jace stopped talking. Nicole's whole life flashed before her. The day her mother left her at that foster home to when she met Ivy. Fast forwarding to when she met Jay, she smiled at all the good times she saw. Tears started flowing when she saw Jace and Ivy together. Holding back the moans she saw when the two guys raped Ivy. She held her stomach when she let Mik beat Jamila's ass. Tightening her teeth she couldn't stomach the sight of her smothering Mrs. May. Tears continued to fall as she saw the sharp knife lunging into Jace's neck. This whole time she had mistaken Jay for Jace and sabotaged her relationships with her close friends. Right then and there she had realized that her mental state had gotten the best of her and it was too late. "Jace you have to believe me, I had mistaken you for your brother. He and I were together before he died. We were suppose to have a baby and get married. Completely ignoring any and everything she had to say, Jace continued on with his speech. "So yeah, I reached out to someone that was close to you and she gave me the green light to do whatever to ya Psycho ass. But the only thing she objected on was me hurting you. She said she'll have the pleasure of doing it herself". Nicole kept pleading with Jace for him to believe her as she kept glancing at Jay's face on the obituary. A sudden noise came from the backseat.

"Hi Nicole! She heard a familiar voice and instantly knew who it was. Nicole felt the cold metal press against the left side of her temple. "Oh bitch you thought you and Mik was gonna just rape and beat me and think it wasn't gonna be consequences?" Jamila spat as she screamed in Nicole's ear. "Answer me!" Nicole couldn't do anything but cry. She was caught red handed and she knew that her time had come. Her last thought was "maybe her and her mom could finally have a relationship in hell!"

Made in the USA
Middletown, DE
30 March 2021